HIGH HOPES AT THE SWEET SHOP OF SECOND CHANCES

HANNAH LYNN

ALSO BY HANNAH LYNN

Standalone Feel Good Novels

The Afterlife of Walter Augustus

Treading Water

Erotic Fiction?

The Complete Peas and Carrots Series

Peas, Carrots and an Aston Martin

Peas, Carrots and a Red Feather Boa

Peas, Carrots and Six More Feet

Peas, Carrots and Lessons in Life

Peas, Carrots and Panic at the Plot

Peas, Carrots and Happily Ever After

The Holly Berry Sweet Shop Series

The Sweet Shop of Second Chances

Romance at the Sweet Shop of Second Chances

Turmoil at the Sweet Shop of Second Chances

High Hopes at the Sweet Shop of Second Chances

The Grecian Women Series

Athena's Child

A Spartan's Sorrow

Queens of Themiscyra

ISBN: 978-1-915346-10-0

Imprint: Independently published
Edited by Victoria Straw
Cover design by Cherie Chapman

For Elsie,

CHAPTER ONE

Holly Berry was sitting on an exceptionally comfy sofa. With its soft round cushions and high back, this wasn't some flat-packed, mass-produced, run-of-the-mill sofa. This was designer. The type of sofa that you could curl up and sleep on all day and all night for a week and not even suffer the slightest crick in the neck. This was absolute luxury. Yet despite all its softness and plump cushions, Holly was exceptionally uncomfortable.

Summer was on the turn, and after a month of scorching days where no amount of fans or air conditioning had been enough to lessen the stifling heat, this week had been substantially milder. They had even been treated to a little rain. But that didn't change the fact that Holly was currently dripping with sweat. Then again, it had nothing to do with the weather, she thought as she cradled her swollen belly.

"So tell me, would you like to continue what we were discussing last week, or are there any new issues that have arisen? The ball is in your court." The woman opposite peered over her glasses as she looked intently between Ben and Holly before finally settling her gaze on Ben.

Holly glanced to her side, where Ben was sitting bolt upright, his shoulders and back rigid, looking almost as awkward as she felt. He cleared his throat a couple of times before turning to Holly.

"I guess. It's up to you," he said. "We should talk about whatever you want to talk about."

It took all Holly's resolve not to bite. Instead, she gritted her teeth. She should have known that Ben would push the focus back on her. That was what he always did. Though, to be fair, that was probably what she would have done had the question been directed at her. Holly and Ben were six months into their sessions with couples counsellor Dr Ellis. Deep down, Holly knew it had helped them both open up about their issues. But at times like this, she really wished she'd never suggested it at all.

"I… I suppose there have been no new issues," said Holly, trying to read the expression on the counsellor's face as she scribbled a few notes on her tablet screen. "No, no new issues at all. It's been a good week, I think. Don't you, Ben?"

"I think so," he added, nodding vigorously in agreement. "I think it's been a very good week."

"Why is that?" Dr Ellis asked, glancing up from her screen to look at Holly. "What's made this week particularly good?"

From the way the woman was staring so pointedly at her, Holly knew she had no choice but to answer the question. And it wasn't that she didn't want to. It was just difficult to know what to say.

"Well, we've had dinner together three nights this week, or maybe four. Was it three or four nights, Ben?" She desperately wanted him to take the reins.

"I think it was four nights," he said.

"Right, four nights. And Ben is still walking me to work each morning," she added hurriedly, thinking that might be something Dr Ellis would award a gold star for. Not that she did things like that. Though maybe she should, Holly thought. Maybe people would sort out their relationship problems more quickly if a sticker chart was involved. Satisfied that she had answered the question well, Holly allowed herself to relax into the cushions, but her muscles had barely loosened when the counsellor hit them with another question. One she really should have seen coming, no matter how much she didn't want to answer it.

"And the intimacy?" Dr Ellis asked. "That's still an issue?" Only the slightest question mark inflected her speech as her gaze moved between the pair of them. At this point, Holly couldn't look up anymore. She couldn't look at the counsellor, and she certainly couldn't look at Ben. So instead, she glanced down at the massive balloon that was now her stomach.

At the beginning of her and Ben's relationship, intimacy hadn't been a problem at all. Unless the problem was how much of it there was. For those first two months, they couldn't keep their hands off one another, which got them into this situation. Holly Berry was pregnant with Ben Thornberry's baby. And while on paper, the pairing really wasn't too bad a match at all—fun, caring, sweet shop owner and hardworking, trustworthy bank manager—seeing things on paper and living them in real life were very different.

"We've been cuddling a lot," Holly said, desperately needing to break the silence swirling around them. "And kissing too. I'd say there was definitely more kissing this week, wouldn't you, Ben?"

She looked at him now, unable to hide the pleading in her voice and eyes. It was time he did some of the talking this session, although she felt a little guilty about throwing that particular question in his direction.

The pregnancy had definitely not been planned. In fact, it had been so unplanned that only days before Holly had discovered she was carrying Ben's child, she had broken the whole relationship off, fearing that Ben was still in love with his ex. Upon finding out that he was about to become a father, Ben had become so overbearingly controlling that Holly threatened to cut him out of the baby's life entirely. But that hadn't lasted long. The truth was that since his tempestuous reaction to discovering Holly was pregnant, Ben had been trying to do everything in his power to make sure this pregnancy went as smoothly as possible.

It was Ben who had read all the terrifying baby books that listed every possible disaster scenario so that Holly didn't have to. He had gone through the list of suitable and unsuitable foods, preparing meal plans so that she didn't have to worry about that. He'd been there with foot massages, on late-night cravings runs, and all this while working all the extra hours the bank could throw at him. Several of the smaller local branches were closing, and while the Bourton branch currently remained, he had taken the leap into personal banking. It had its plus sides; more flexible hours that would help when the baby came, not to mention the extra money. But he was at the beck and call of the clients, meaning he had to travel here, there, and everywhere, sometimes with only a couple of days' notice. Simply put, he was doing everything he could do to make her happy and more.

"Well, kissing is definitely a good thing," Dr Ellis said, breaking the silence, although Holly couldn't help but notice that Ben had stayed quiet on the matter. Now that she thought of it, there had been a couple of times in the week when she'd pulled away from him. When they'd been watching a film on the sofa, the kissing got a little too intense. But then, what did he expect? She was eight months pregnant. She could barely even manoeuvre herself to get into the car. Surely he understood that any antics in the bedroom were off the cards for a little while, at least. Besides, he'd not put her in the best mood earlier in the evening when he had commented on how all the sugar she was eating could put the baby at risk and had therefore cleared out all sugary foods from his cupboards, apparently overlooking the fact that Holly owned a sweet shop.

"Ben, Holly's done a lot of talking this session," Dr Ellis said, finally giving Holly her deserved dues. "Why don't you tell me how you're feeling? Is there anything you feel Holly could do to help you feel more secure in this relationship?"

The relief that Holly had felt at having the attention taken away from her immediately evaporated. These were the type of questions that caused her stomach to flip and her chest to tighten. Somehow, it was even worse when Ben answered them than when she did.

"Ahh," Ben let out a long sigh that blew like a heavy gust of wind between them. Even when it was done, he took another deep inhale before he actually said something. "I guess I still feel the same that I've felt since we started the sessions. That Holly's holding back from me."

"And why do you think that is?"

"I don't know. I don't know what more I can do."

Dr Ellis nodded a few more times, although rather than jotting anything down on her tablet, she was already straight back at Holly with the next question.

"So, what can you say to Ben about how he's feeling, Holly?"

The room was shrinking in on her as two sets of eyes bored

into her. How many times had she answered this exact same question in this exact same room in front of these exact same people? She wanted to scream at them. Ten? Twenty? A hundred? It certainly felt like that. So why was she still asking the same question? In the pit of her annoyance, guilt flickered within her. She knew exactly why she was being asked again. Because the truth was, she probably was holding back. She just didn't want to admit it.

"We had broken up," Holly said, unable to hide the exasperation in her voice. "And some of the things he did and said made me… I don't know… wary, I guess."

"But you want to be with Ben now?"

"Of course I want to be with Ben now."

"Because you love him?"

There had been a time when it had been so easy to say. When the words had been desperate to jump off her tongue, well before she knew about the baby, they had said it to each other since. The night Ben wrote a letter explaining everything he had gone through in a previous relationship, he had professed his deepest, truest feelings to her. She had told him she loved him then. And in the weeks that followed. But for some reason, it had got harder and harder with time, and those words were forming on her lips much less often, if at all, over these past few weeks. And it wasn't meant to be that way, was it? Surely it was meant to get easier to tell someone you loved them, not more difficult. So what did it mean? A little thought flickered in the back of her mind, but she pushed it down as far as she could.

"I… I am terrified of being hurt," she answered, the only truth she could give. "I am terrified of what the future holds. Right now, all I can think about is how I will keep my business and my life together with the baby. That's all I have space for in my head."

"And you think loving Ben will take up more space?" Dr Ellis tipped her head to the side quizzically, eyeing Holly with increased curiosity. "How do you think taking this last little leap of faith would change things? You're already in a relationship together, aren't you?"

A lump had formed in Holly's throat. A thick and obstructive lump that didn't want to let her speak. She attempted to clear her throat, blinking as she felt the prick of tears start to burn behind her eyes. She wasn't going to do this; she wouldn't cry here again. She swallowed and then opened her mouth, unsure what she was even going to say, when Ben took her hand and squeezed tightly.

"Don't worry," he said, his eyes solely on her. "There's no rush with this. I'm not going anywhere."

Holly smiled, squeezing his hand back with all the strength she could muster, though it still wasn't enough to stop that ache from spreading through her chest.

CHAPTER TWO

By the time they finished their counselling session, Holly felt like she had gone through a mental marathon. It was always this way. Utterly exhausting and emotionally draining. The single hour on Dr Ellis's comfy sofa left her feeling crappy and crabby. But she was the one who said they had to do this if they were going to give this relationship a real go. And she stood by that. There was no denying that she and Ben were talking much more about their feelings, past relationships, and what would happen when the baby came. She had learned more about him and the inner workings of his mind in the last couple of months of counselling than she had after years with her ex-boyfriend, Dan, but there were just a few sticking points. That was all.

"Right, I guess I should go do the food shop now," Holly said. This had become their routine in the last weeks. Since Stow-on-the-Wold was smack between Moreton-in-Marsh, where they had their counselling sessions, and Bourton-on-the-Water, where there was the biggest supermarket in the region, it made sense for Holly to get her weekly shop in straight after the sessions.

"Why don't I come with you?" Ben said. "I'm sure I can spare another half an hour. And I don't like the idea of you carrying all those heavy bags alone."

"The bags are no heavier than the ones at the shop," Holly insisted. "Besides, if you take time off now, you'll end up working late into the evening, and you don't want to do that. Honestly, it's fine. I'm sure if anything's too heavy, I can ask someone who works there to pick it up."

"Okay, as long as you're sure?"

He leant over as if to kiss her, only to duck down, place both his hands on her belly, and place a kiss right on the top of her bump. "Be a good little thing for Mummy, okay? Don't cause her too much stress." When he stood up, he planted a light kiss on the corner of Holly's lips before turning and getting into the car.

Holly followed him all the way down the Fosseway to Stow, at which point Ben carried straight on to Bourton, and Holly turned left into the supermarket. After parking, she pulled out the shopping list carefully curated by Ben for this, her third trimester of pregnancy. Obviously, alcohol was no longer allowed, but he had also insisted she limit her amount of oily fish, switch to decaf coffee and tea and drink a maximum of two cups of herbal tea a day. Then there was the sugar situation.

Given the sweetshop, there was very little Ben could do to erase sugar from her diet entirely, but he had *suggested* that she not bring home quite as many packets of fudge and coconut ice as she used to. By which he meant none. And he suggested she limit her baking to more savoury items, so she wasn't too tempted. That was one of the reasons Holly preferred to do the food shop alone. If Ben was with her, it took four times longer as he Googled everything she picked up to check the macro, salt, and additive content and decide whether it was a good idea for her and the baby. And she could sneak in a packet of crisps in the car on the way home, too.

Holly slung her handbag over her shoulder and ambled towards the shop entrance, practically salivating over the prospect of purchasing a scotch egg or some other type of savoury contraband. She dug in her bag to find a coin when she reached the trolleys.

One of her bugbears about shopping here was the fact that the trolleys were chained together, only to be released with a pound coin. Of course, she found it such a bugbear because she could never find a coin when she needed one. Two minutes later, she was still digging about in the depths of her handbag. What was ridiculous was with the size of her bag, there simply had to be a pound coin in there. There was everything else in there; a hairbrush, a water bottle, a small bottle of deodorant, a phone charger, at least three pens, five hair ties, a thousand receipts, and goodness knows what else. She was digging about in the small side pockets, pulling out handfuls of coppers and a couple of rather squished Fruit Salad Chews, when a voice spoke behind her.

"I honestly do not understand why you don't just keep a coin in your bag for this. Is it that hard to remember? You come here every week."

The corner of Holly's lips twitched with a smile, although she managed to suppress it and replace it with a glower as she turned around. Behind her, dressed in a salmon pink shirt and wearing his most withering look, was Giles Caverty.

"Well, isn't this a coincidence?" she said dryly.

CHAPTER THREE

"Mind out of the way," Giles said, placing his hands on either side of Holly's shoulders and shifting her half a foot to the left. "This is too painful to watch." Having manoeuvred Holly to the side of the trolley, he took a pound from his pocket and slipped it into the trolley, releasing the chain and freeing it for her. "Right. What's on the shopping list today? How many things has he banned you from having this week?"

Holly pulled the trolley out without speaking and dropped her handbag into the bottom. She turned it around to face the shop entrance, then threw a glance over her shoulder back at Giles.

"Are you coming? I don't have all day. I need to get back to the shop."

"How could I refuse an offer like that?"

The truth was, meeting Giles while doing her weekly food shop like this had been entirely coincidental. At least the first couple of times they had done it. Despite being a snake that nearly cost Holly her sweetshop, she and Giles had reconnected back when Holly had first discovered she was pregnant. And his response had been overwhelmingly sweet when he sent her a care package full of antenatal vitamins and non-alcoholic wine. Since then, he had been there with the occasional text message, just checking how she was doing and if there was anything she needed. And these meetings, which, while initially accidental, had proved as regular as her and Ben's trip to Dr Ellis. Not that Ben knew anything about it. Given his and Giles' general animosity towards one another, there was no chance Ben would take kindly to the news that the pair were strolling the aisles at Tesco together, even if it mainly did involve looking at the best offers on vegetable medleys.

"You're very quiet today," Giles said as he picked up a basket, keeping his step in time with Holly's. "I take it the session with the shrink didn't go well?"

"It's not a shrink," Holly told him. "It's a couples counsellor."

"Aren't they the same thing?"

Ignoring him, Holly pushed her trolley through the automatic doors, the chill of air conditioning hitting her in a blast.

"I'm not in a bad mood," she said, eventually. "I'm just thinking, that's all."

"About the bank manager?"

"Sort of," Holly admitted. "About a lot of things."

She paused in front of the first aisle where they stacked the biggest offers and picked up a packet of washing powder. It probably wouldn't meet Ben's specifications for the baby clothes, but it would do for her things. Anything she could do to help save pennies at that moment was worth it. She dropped it into her trolley and was about to move on when she spotted a woman placing a large tray of tasters onto small table.

With what was probably her most decisive movement of the

day, Holly left Giles where he was standing, and marched over to the forest of cocktail stick flags each planted into a sample of cheese.

"Can I help myself?" Holly said to the lady.

"Of course dear. They're all rather good, but personally, I think the Wensleydale is exceptional."

Following the woman's advice, Holly picked out a flag with Wensleydale written on it and popped the cheese in her mouth.

"Oh wow," Holly said from behind her hand as she chewed. "This is good."

After testing each of the four cheeses on offer, Holly agreed that the Wensleydale was probably her favourite too and was helping herself to another piece when Giles came up behind her, clearly determined to continue their previous conversation.

"I don't know why you don't tell him," he said. "We do our supermarket shop at the same time. It's not like anything's going on. I don't think it's physically possible, is it? With a bump that size? Urgh." He mock-shuddered, then threw her a sideways glance, displaying his characteristic smirk. Holly couldn't help but smile, no matter how much she didn't want to.

"You know you are a completely shallow arse, don't you?"

"I hear some people find that utterly charming."

Holly moved from the Wensleydale back to the Edam and the pair fell into silence again, which Holly assumed would be broken when Giles risked another joke at her expense, but instead, he came out with something unexpectedly serious.

"I think I should speak to Ben. Not about us. This… whatever this is. I need to talk to him about the old people's home. He's on my list."

Giles' list. At first, Holly had thought it was some kind of scary ploy to deviate from how truly evil he'd been to her, but the more she saw and spoke to him, the more she saw it was the truth. For the last six months, he had been trying to make amends for his past actions. Trying to repair his reputation and standing in the village and maybe gain a bit of forgiveness. And while Holly didn't think she'd ever be able to forgive him for what he had put her through, she knew there wasn't much more he could do to prove he had changed.

"And I think you should tell him about these little rendezvous too. I'm starting to think you're ashamed of being seen with me."

Holly scoffed as she reached for another cheese sample. Given that the Wensleydale was definitely better than the Edam and other two samples, she didn't want to finish on the wrong one. "You *know* I'm ashamed of being seen with you," she said dropping six cocktail sticks in the waste tub at once.

"I take it you like that one, dear?" said the lady with what appeared to be a rather tight smile.

"Oh, it's delicious."

"Then perhaps you want to leave some for other people to try?" Giles commented.

Holly wasn't blind to the fact that almost all her non-verbal communication with Giles consisted of her glaring at him, but that didn't stop her from shooting him yet another glower.

"Well, I'm glad I gave up an extra hour on the shoot for this riveting conversation," he countered back at her.

This was how they generally spoke to each other, exchanging one insult and then another. It was a long way from the smart sycophantic Giles who constantly sucked up to her as he tried to get information on the shop. And as it happened, Holly much preferred this version of him.

"Well, if you feel my conversation is that dull, why don't you tell me something you'd like to talk about?" Holly said. Her hand stretched back out for more cheese.

"Okay, I will." Giles said, fixing her with a look. But it wasn't the usual look that he gave her, joking, friendly. Instead, this was an intense stare that she could feel boring all the way through her as he bit down slightly on his bottom lip.

"Go on then," Holly countered popping yet more cheese into her mouth. "What do you want to talk about?" She turned back to the cheese platter only to do a double take.

The table, that she had happily been helping herself from had mysteriously moved over by two or three feet and the woman had positioned herself between Holly and the cheese. Swivelling her trolly around, Holly marched back over the table, where she offered her best passive aggressive smile before whipping her hand out for one more piece of cheese. She was still chewing on it when Giles spoke again.

"Why don't we talk about why you should leave Ben and be with me instead?"

An involuntary half-cough half-gasp escaped from Holly's mouth, along with a small piece of Wensleydale cheese.

CHAPTER FOUR

It felt like the cool air had been sucked out of the store and replaced by an infernal heat. Holly was used to feeling overheated. Being pregnant in the middle of summer did that, but this was something entirely different. This was not that sort of heat. These meetings with Giles had been nothing but platonic. Or at least that was what she had told herself repeatedly. Yes, he had mentioned wanting to take her to meet his sister again a couple of times, and also mentioned wanting to sweep her off abroad. But in her mind, all those comments had been said in jest. But now she was looking at him and there wasn't a hint of his trademark humour on his lips.

Holly gripped the trolley in front of her, only half aware of the people trying to reach around her to get a punnet of raspberries.

"My god, you are easy to wind up, Berry," Giles said, reaching across to pick up a punnet for himself, and dropping them into his basket. "As if I could deal with you and all your drama. Jeez, not to mention a baby. No, thank you. I think I'll stay well clear of that."

"You really are an arse. You know that, don't you?" Holly said, the gasp of relief blowing from her lungs.

The corkscrewing smile on his face showed the great pleasure that he had gained from Holly's discomfort, and for that split second she wondered how she had ever considered Giles relationship material. There was quite possibly no man in the world who was less relationship material than he was. He was, however, a fun friend, and the time sped past as he talked about trips to Monaco and vintage sport cars that he was thinking of investing in. Still, they ambled around the shop contently, him filling his basket with frivolous things, like artichoke hearts and smoked salmon, while Holly displayed all the exciting parts of her life, with items like washing up liquid and toilet rolls. They were just about to reach the till when Giles stopped her, grabbing her by the forearm.

"Hold on a second, don't move," he said

"Why?"

"I said just stay still for a minute, will you?"

Holly had thought it was simply another opportunity for Giles to wind her up when his hand reached up towards her hair. A twisting of nerves rippled through her as his fingers skimmed against the side of her cheek. Was he going to kiss her? Her mind screamed out to her. No, surely not. That would be ridiculous. He couldn't kiss her here in a supermarket. Or anywhere, for that matter. She was with Ben. He knew she was with Ben. Still, her throat was closing in, and a swarm of butterflies threatened to send her into early labour. She should say something, she thought to herself, when his hand swept outwards.

"Your earring, it's come out," he said.

"It has?"

He plucked the offending item from where it had caught in

her hair. As he withdrew his hand, there in the palm was a gold stud. It was far larger than Holly would have normally chosen to wear, and bolder too, with a bright green stone in the centre, but they were a gift from Ben, so she wore them most days.

"Where is the back?" she said as her hand went up to her ear to feel for the butterfly that held the earrings in place. Quickly realising it wasn't there, she brushed through her hair, looking on the ground to see if anything fell, but it didn't.

"You must have lost it somewhere in the shop," Giles said. "Do you want me to go look? I don't know what the chances of finding it are though, you're probably better off buying a new one."

Holly continued to scour the ground by her feet for a moment longer before releasing an annoyed sigh.

"No, it's probably gone," she said, still pouting, despite being thankful she hadn't lost the earring.

"Are you going to take this, or am I supposed to stand here holding your earring like some kind of handmaid?" Giles' voice brought her back to the moment.

"Sorry."

Hurriedly, Holly plucked the earring from the palm of his hand, although at this point she found herself stuck. Her dress had no pockets, and her handbag was right at the bottom of the trolley beneath salad leaves, chicken fillets and three dozen other packets, cans and tins.

"Here, give it back to me," Giles said, taking it back and dropping it into the top pocket of his shirt. "I guess I've just been promoted to your porter now."

Holly smiled gratefully. "I think being a porter requires a little more work than you're used to," she said with a smirk.

At the cashier, Giles loaded her bags back into the trolley, then paid for his own purchases.

"I don't suppose I can tempt you with a coffee before you have to jet off, can I?" he asked casually when they reached the carpark and he unloaded the contents of the trolley into the back of the car. Holly avoided his eyes as she replied.

"I've got to get back to the shop," she said. "And I need to unpack all of this first."

Giles' head bobbed up and down rapidly in a nod. "I get it. It's no problem. Well, I'll probably be doing my shopping around the same time next week. Who knows, perhaps I'll bump into you again then?"

"Perhaps," Holly replied. "Although I don't know."

"Of course not."

"This was nice. A nice coincidence," she added, the heat of earlier rapidly returning. At her words, Giles' eyes glinted.

"It's probably my favourite coincidence of the week," he smirked.

That was it. That was as much as Holly could cope with. She could feel the burning redness of her cheeks. The tightness in her throat travelling down and clamping around her throat.

Leaving the trolley for Giles to deal with, she jumped into her car, switched on the engine and dropped her hands into her lap.

What the hell she was doing, supermarket shopping with a man she was supposed to hate? It was the pregnancy hormones. It had to be. Didn't it?

CHAPTER FIVE

By the time Holly had put away the groceries and got back to the shop, it was nearly four, and only an hour left until they would close for the day. Still, *Just One More* was a hive of activity. While Caroline ran around the shop floor, hopping on and off the stepladder as she grabbed one jar of sweets, then another, Holly's dad, Arthur, was on the till weighing up and bagging the sweets like an old-hand. Over the last few months, Mr Berry had managed to find the fine line between a friendly exchange with a customer and eliciting their entire life story. She had to give it to her dad. He really was an asset to the shop.

That said, on quiet days he could still spend a full half hour chatting away to the regular customers about an upcoming football match, or the weather in certain areas of Europe if left unchecked, but on a day-to-day basis he was a star. Since she had taken him on, he had worked every day she had asked him, and his flexibility had been an absolute godsend when it came to things like doctors' appointments. Not to mention these weekly counselling sessions.

"Do you need a hand?" Holly said, squeezing through the teeming customers to get to her dad. "What can I do to help?"

"I don't think there's enough room back here for you, me and the bump," he said, indicating behind the counter. "Why don't you go upstairs and put the kettle on, make us all a brew? It's been like this for over an hour. Six coaches arrived after you left. Six!"

Holly watched on as men, women, and children grabbed bags of lemon bonbons and sticks of rock.

"Caroline?" Holly said, feeling like she should do something to help. "Anything I can do?"

"Don't worry about us. We've got a rhythm. A cup of tea would be a lifesaver, though."

Sensing that her presence was more of a hindrance than a help, Holly did as she was asked and trudged up the stairs, gripping the bannister to keep her steady. Upstairs, as she filled the kettle, she wondered if there were other establishments where the boss was sent upstairs to make the tea while the rest of the workers scurried about downstairs doing the actual work. In the end, she decided it didn't really matter either way. They were a team that worked together well, and they were lucky to have one another.

Hearing that the shop was still brimming with people, Holly waited a minute before she flicked on the kettle. After all, there was no point making them tea if they weren't going to be able to drink it while it was hot. Instead, she reached for her handbag and pulled out her phone. She had switched it off during her counselling session with Ben. As such, when she turned it on, it buzzed several times with messages, all of which were from her antenatal group, and she had no intention of reading them. Those women had way too much time on their hands.

"Brill, you're here," said a voice coming up the stairs.

Drey was the fourth and final member of the *Just One More* team, and despite being the youngest, technically speaking, she had been there the longest. She had been working for Maud, Holly's original employer, before Holly bought the shop and was pretty much responsible for not letting it turn to ruin. Back then, she had worked far more hours than a teenager probably should have done. Maud hadn't even had the funds to pay her, but now she had enrolled at the local college and normally just worked at the weekends.

"I wanted to remind you I'm not here this weekend," she said, leaning against the wall, and dropping a large canvas bag on to the ground. Drey's fashion was as variable as the English weather, and over the eighteen months that Holly had known her, she had gone through more metamorphoses than a caterpillar, but that day denim was the chosen form of attire. Her denim mini skirt and denim jacket were teamed with black boots and a denim head band that was wrapped around her dip-dyed pink hair. "I won't be back until Sunday night. So I can't do either day."

"It's all on the calendar," Holly said, tapping the A3 planner on the wall behind her. In truth, Holly hadn't expected Drey to still be there working with them. But her exams the previous year had not gone as well as she had expected, or needed, and so rather than disappearing off to university, she had stayed close to home and was completing an Arts Foundation course. She seemed perfectly happy with the current situation, but from her comments about her father, Holly suspected Drey's parents were less than happy with the turn of events.

With Drey's lectures and coursework, Holly's appointments and Caroline's childcare commitments, organisation was the key to keeping the place running. Organisation she was going to need even more of when the baby came. "Dad and I are both in, and Caroline is on backup, should we need anyone extra. You are definitely one hundred percent free. So go, have fun. Enjoy yourself. You still haven't told me what you've got planned."

Generally, Drey displayed substantially fewer teenage characteristics than when Holly had first met her, yet the shrug she responded with reminded Holly of that goth loving girl she had wrongly accused of shoplifting when they first met.

"You know, this and that," she replied. "London stuff."

"Sounds great," Holly laughed, before recalling something and cutting herself short. "You're not driving, are you?" she said.

"No, why?"

"I think Ben said something about protests going on. Road closures and tail backs are expected this weekend, I think."

"Oh no," Drey said, shaking her head. "No, we're taking the train up. Should be fine."

"Great, and don't worry about us. We'll be fine."

Given that she had said what she came to say, Holly expected Drey to head back downstairs, but instead her eyes went to Holly's belly before lifting back up to meet her eyes.

"Everything go okay with therapy and the bank manager today?" she asked.

Holly pressed her lips together. "It's not therapy, it's couples counselling."

"Is there even a difference?"

Holly sighed. She should probably admit she didn't actually know, or at least look the up differences online. "Yes, everything is fine between Ben and me, thank you. We are fine. I am fine. Ben is fine."

This time it was Drey who pursed her lips, twisting them as

if she was sucking on a super sour. Drey and Holly had had plenty of heart to hearts over the last year or so. It was hard not to when they spent so much time together. It helped, having a younger, more opinionated outlook sometimes. Besides, Caroline and Jamie were both incredibly close to Ben and were desperate for a fairy-tale happy ending to come true, while Holly's parents were just so worried about everything, that Holly didn't dare say anything remotely negative. Drey was always brutally honest about what she thought, no matter how much Holly didn't always want to hear it.

"Fine," Drey responded with an eye roll. "That's a great word to describe the man you're about to have a baby with. Not brilliant. Not incredible. Fine."

Holly knew what game she was playing at, and she didn't want to bite, but the counselling session and the fact that she had a watermelon strapped to her abdomen made it harder not to snap.

"Fine, is good," she said. "When you get to my age, fine is absolutely acceptable. Lots of people don't get fine. Lots of people long for fine."

"Your age?" Drey said, raising her eyebrows. "You know you only turned thirty a couple of months ago? And besides, I don't care about other people. I care about you. And *fine*, is not good enough for you. You need someone who makes you feel how Eddy makes me feel." At the name of her boyfriend, Drey fluttered her eyelids. Though she'd never said it out loud, there was no doubt that Eddy was another reason Drey was less than devastated at not heading straight to university. While this hadn't been the first relationship Drey had told Holly about, it was the longest, and Drey was obviously smitten. Holly, however, remained quiet on the matter. Although Drey talked about him non-stop, Holly was yet to meet the illusive Eddy. But at twenty-five there was a seven-year age gap between him and Drey, and Holly was concerned that Drey was setting herself up for heartbreak. But then again, what person got through life without having their heart broken at least once?

"Look, just make sure you are following your heart," Drey said. "You know it's only going to end badly if you don't."

If Holly had got the strength to heave herself out of her seat, she would have hugged Drey, but given that she had only just sat herself down, she didn't quite feel up to it, emotionally or physically. Instead, she simply smiled.

"You have a great weekend, and don't get into any trouble," she said.

"Me?" Drey smirked indignantly. "As if."

Laughing, Drey picked up her bag and disappeared downstairs, leaving Holly on her own with her thoughts. *Fine* was okay, wasn't it? Everything she had said to Drey was true. *Fine* was all some people longed for. In fact, half the world's problems probably stemmed from people wanting more than just *fine*. From people who were never satisfied with their life the way it was. And she wasn't one of those people. She knew when she had got something good, and Ben was something good. That was what she kept having to remind herself. Particularly when he got all controlling. It was a couple of minutes later she realised she could no longer hear the ringing of the till and the chattering of people down in the shop. A second after she had realised the shop was quiet, her father's voice rang up from down below.

"Are you making that tea?" he called.

With a hundred thoughts still whirring around her mind, Holly pushed herself onto her feet and moved over to the small kitchenette and flicked on the kettle.

"Just coming," she said.

CHAPTER SIX

Another major change that had occurred since Holly purchased *Just One More* was how much she saw of her parents. In fact, she hadn't seen this much of them since she had lived at home over a decade before. Part of it came from her dad working more and more hours at the shop. What had started as two days a week had increased to include the weekend too, and other weekdays, when she needed a bit more support. As such, she often gave him a lift home, so he didn't have to catch the bus and mostly when she did that, she ended up staying for dinner with her parents, and her mother made no attempt to hide how much this pleased her.

"Well, this is a surprise," Wendy said as Holly appeared in the kitchen behind her dad.

"Now tell me, do you want something to eat? I've just put a pie in the oven, and there's more than enough. I could put some more potatoes on for the mash too if you want? But that won't be for another hour. There's some fresh rhubarb cake in the tin if you'd like that instead?"

"And double cream in the fridge too," Arthur piped up, already opening up

"Pie and mash sounds perfect," Holly replied.

"Fabulous. Do you want to go upstairs and have a quick shower? You've got some clean clothes in the spare room, then you can put your feet up until dinner's ready. And you can tell me all about how today's session with the therapist went."

Holly gritted her teeth. She didn't mind that her friends and family knew she and Ben were seeing the counsellor together, but there were only so many times in a day when she could nod and smile and say that the sessions were going fine. Thankfully, her dad read the situation.

"Leave the poor girl alone, Wendy. Come on Hols, try a slice of this cake," he said, pouring over a healthy dose of cream.

For a split second Wendy looked as though she was going to say something, when she shook her head and sighed.

"Don't you go ruining your appetite for dinner," she said instead.

Despite sort of living with Ben she kept her room at Jamie's house and enjoyed spending a couple of nights a week there. Friday night was one of those nights. It was only when she pulled up outside her neighbouring homes that Holly remembered Fin, Jamie's live-in boyfriend, was cooking a meal that night. And when Fin cooked a meal, he cooked a meal. Fighting back the annoyance at herself for forgetting and having a second helping of her mum's chicken and mushroom pie. She opened her front door and was immediately assaulted by an aromatic wall of spices, so strong they caught in the back of her throat. Before pregnancy, she had never been fussed about spicy food, and would happily take it or leave it, but every month her love of curries had increased. She had tried the spiciest things from all the local takeaways, devouring dishes that left Ben's eyes watering from just a sniff, and so now Fin had taken up the challenge of trying to hit the mark with the spiciest dishes he could manage. Normally Holly had no problems going in for seconds, or even thirds, but today she was already full up. She'd just have to have a small bowl to begin, and then hopefully, given the way her appetite was at the minute, she'd be ready for another helping soon enough.

"There you are," Jamie said, as Holly stepped into the kitchen. "I was starting to worry about you."

"Sorry," Holly said. "I just went to Mum and Dad's for a bit. You know, just checking in with them. Mum never believes dad when he says I'm doing fine."

"Well, you're home just in time. Fin's about to dish up. I didn't know if Ben was coming over too?"

"No, not tonight. You know, individual space and all that. Besides, he wanted to get the nursery painted."

"Everything okay with the counsellor today?" Jamie asked the inevitable question, to which Holly mumbled her typical answer.

"Everything was fine."

After changing into her slippers, Holly slid into a seat around the kitchen table. At the hob, Fin was busy stirring a large pan which was sizzling away and responsible for filling the room with scented steam. It smelt even more delicious close up than it had out in the hallway, but apparently not everything with going quite to plan.

"Oh crap," he muttered, half under his breath.

"Everything alright, baby?" Jamie moved across to Fin, where she rested a hand on his shoulder to peer at the dish. To say Holly hadn't been sure about Fin and Jamie's relationship was an understatement. And she had had reasons to be sceptical. Things had moved so fast. She had barely even heard about him before they were going off on holiday together and then he was moving in, with his hippy, chilled, Californian ways. Yet her fears were unfounded. As it happened, he wasn't the scrounging, unscrupulous, money-grabbing conman she feared he was. In fact, he was an incredibly successful skateboarder who had started his own business designing bespoke skateboards and sold it for more money than she would probably earn in the lifetime. And now he lived here with them, in a semi-detached house in the Cotswolds, content with making origami cranes and cooking them dinners inspired by his travels.

"What's wrong with it? It looks amazing," Jamie said, looking at the food.

"I forgot to get the coriander," Fin said with a shake of his head.

"Oh, there're loads in the garden," Holly joined in the conversation. "Do you need me to go get a bunch?"

Despite her offer, Fin threw her a look, implying he was anything but pleased by Holly's suggestion.

"It's not just the coriander, I forgot the limes, too. The flavour balance of the entire meal is going to be completely off if I don't have limes in it."

Fin was the calmest, most collected guy Holly knew. So laid back that he made whale music sound like hip-hop. Yet he looked uncharacteristically flustered. And Holly wasn't the only one to notice.

"I'm sure it will be great," Jamie said, taking his hand and squeezing it. Still, Fin didn't look convinced.

"Would I be the worst boyfriend in the world if I asked you to go?" he said. "I'd go myself, only, if the coconut milk gets too hot and boils, then it'll split and then the entire meal will lose its consistency which isn't really what I want."

Holly was about to suggest that she could keep an eye on it, and Fin could go to the shop, but Jamie was already on her tip-toes giving him a farewell peck on the cheek.

"You know you're the luckiest guy in the whole world, don't you?"

"I never doubted it for a second," he replied, pulling her back in for another kiss before she could get too far away from him.

Holly averted her eyes, well aware that a massive public display of affection was about to occur. To give them their dues, it probably wasn't that public, given it was their own house, but still. She busied herself with her phone until she heard Jamie's footsteps heading across the kitchen.

"Okay, I guess I'll be back in a minute. Anything you want from the shop while I'm out?" Jamie asked Holly. There was no chance Holly could possibly manage any more food, but being pregnant had come with a lot of expenses and afflictions she hadn't considered before. It wasn't just the fact that she had gone up three bra sizes or had had morning sickness well past the twelve week mark. She also had the joy of almost constant heartburn and acid reflux. Given how many meals she was going to enjoy that night, it seemed more than likely that she was going to be suffering badly by the time she went to bed.

"Could you pick me up some antacid?" she said. "The biggest bottle you can find. Extra strength if they have it."

"Oh the glamour of pregnancy," Jamie laughed before blowing Fin another kiss and saying, "I hope you're taking note of all this." A moment later, the front door slammed shut and Fin dropped the wooden spoon in his hand.

"Thank god, I thought she would never go."

"I thought you said you needed to keep stirring that?" Holly said. Knowing a fresh supply of antacids were going to be on hand, nothing was going to stop her enjoying Fin's curry, although he seemed to have forgotten about the importance of maintaining its constant temperature entirely as he raced up the stairs, his thundering footsteps making Holly wonder if she had missed something important.

Less than a minute later and the footsteps were thundering back down.

"Right, I need to show you something, and you can't say anything. And then I need you to find somewhere in your room to hide this, where Jamie definitely won't find it, but I need to know where it is just in case I need to get it when you're not here." He was talking exceptionally fast, and his relaxed demeanour had been replaced by bouncing on his feet. As if standing still for a moment would cause him to explode.

"Is everything alright?" Holly asked.

"Everything's great. Better than great. It's perfect. Which is why I need you to find somewhere to hide this."

CHAPTER SEVEN

"Are you sure you're allowed to tell me this? I feel like this is something you shouldn't be telling me?" Caroline sounded nervous on the other end of the phone.

"Trust me. I'm allowed. I asked Fin explicitly. I used the exact words, *can I tell Caroline?* And he said as long as Michael doesn't find out. Which is fair enough. You know what your husband is like with keeping secrets."

Saturday morning had gone by in a blink, and for once Holly's mind was occupied with things other than her own future. Fin had a ring. Not just any ring.

"You've never seen anything like it," she carried on, before Caroline could get a word in edgeways. "Fin said it was his grandmother's. It has to be at least two carats and with all these little side diamonds. I've no idea how Jamie's going to wear it, but he says he'll get her another one for everyday wear."

"Jeez…" Caroline let out a long breath. "How am I supposed to keep that from Michael?"

"Well you did such a great job last time you had a secret," Holly spoke with mock annoyance. It was because Caroline had told Michael that Holly was pregnant that he had ended up inadvertently informing everyone else at Jamie's birthday. But this wasn't like that. "Seriously though, you need to keep this quiet. He's got this whole big thing planned for the proposal, though he wouldn't tell me what it is or when it is happening."

"Wow."

A pause drifted between the pair of them. Jamie was going to get engaged. Jamie, the eternal bachelorette, was going to get married. And it was happening fast.

"How long have they been together?" Caroline said, replicating Holly's exact thoughts. "Six months. Eight?"

"I guess about that."

"Wow… well, when you know you know, right?" Caroline's words caused an unexpected pang in Holly's chest. Was that really the case? And if it was, then what did it say about all the doubts swimming in her head about her and Ben? No. She shook her head. She refused to think like that now. It was very nice for these instant, love at first sight type people, but some relationships were just more realistic than that. She was excited for Jamie and the fact she had found a great guy who truly loved her. This was amazing news.

"I better get back downstairs. The shop's getting busy and I don't want Dad to get snowed under."

"No problem, I've told Michael I'm on cover should you need me today."

"Great, and remember, not a word to him. Fin would kill me if he blabbed."

After hanging up the phone, Holly waddled down to the shop floor, where her dad was working on a steady queue of people, almost all of whom seemed to be after clotted cream fudge. It was a good job she was in her final trimester, she thought as she squeezed behind the counter. She had developed a proper waddle now.

At three-thirty, during an unusual Saturday afternoon lull, a familiar face appeared in the doorway.

"Hey?" Holly had been giving her feet a break by sitting on the small stool that they used to reach higher jars. It had felt like a good idea at the time, but as she tried to push herself back up to standing, she wondered if it had been a mistake.

"What are you doing?" Ben said, darting over and hooking his arm under her elbow. "I'm sure that can't be good for the baby, not to mention all the extra pressure you're putting on your back, too. I told you that you should get a chair down here."

"This is a nice surprise," Holly said, ignoring the fact that Ben had come straight in and started mothering her.

"Well I missed you," Ben said. "And I wanted to know what time we're planning on leaving tonight. And whether you want to get dinner before or after?"

"Before or after what?" Holly said when a wave of nausea that had nothing to do with the baby hit her. "It's antenatal class today. I'd forgotten. Do I have to go?"

"Only if you want to learn how to keep our child alive. I guess it's optional," Ben said with a fleeting grin that didn't make Holly feel any better.

"The other mothers, they're all just so…"

"Organised?"

"I was going to say perfect, but whatever. You know, last time they spent thirty minutes after the session, discussing how often they go for their prenatal massages and what essential oils they use that help to de-stress the baby."

"Well, if you find out which oils work, I'll be more than

happy to give you the massage," Ben grinned. "I'm more than happy to get my hands a bit greasy for you."

Holly felt herself blushing and turned deliberately away from where her dad was still busy at the till.

"How about I find out the oils and we skip the class?" Holly tried.

Ben released a short chuckle. "Nice try. There's no getting out of this, I'm afraid."

"Fine."

Deep down, Holly knew she had to go. The fact was she had zero experience in child rearing. Less than zero probably. She didn't even have a baby cousin or a nephew or niece to help her prepare. In fact, Ben was much more knowledgeable about the whole thing. Which was probably why his sister, Jess, had insisted on paying for these exclusive sessions just outside of Cold Aston. The complex played host to a gym, spa and large barn conversion used as a wedding venue and the entire place dripped money. In Holly's opinion holding antenatal classes in a room with floor to ceiling mirrors, where you were forced to sit in the most unflattering angles and watch as your belly grew exponentially, was basically the gyms way of ensuring they had a steady stream of new sign-ups. But it wasn't just the mirrors or the fact that Holly would have never been able to pay for it on her own that made her uneasy. Nor was it because of how much more the other parents seemed to know about pregnancy in general.

It was a couples' class, with mothers and their partners attending. And whether it was a strange statistical anomaly or not, these couples all doted upon one another. Only one other couple besides Ben and Holly weren't married—but they had been together for nearly ten years. There were two women who ran their businesses together and seemed totally in sync with each other, a couple who had known each other since primary school and another who apparently experienced love at first sight in a manner worthy of a Richard Curtis film. Being thrust into an environment where she was surrounded by such perfect relationships made Holly uncomfortable, particularly when she and Ben weren't even living together full time.

"So, dinner before or after?" Ben said, prompting Holly out of her daydream.

"After," she said. "I can never manage all the stretches when I'm bloated."

"After it is. I'll come back here at five, then I can walk you home."

"You don't have to do that."

"I know I don't, but I want to."

Comments like that used to warm her heart, but now it was hard not to think he was just doing it so he could monitor her and the baby. Still, Holly made herself think about all the discussions they had had with Dr Ellis. He loved her. He really loved her. "That would be nice," she said, holding her smile and meaning it. "I should get back to work now, though."

"Of course, I'll see you later then."

"See you later."

"Looking forward to it." A second later, he was gone and Holly was trying to imagine all the dreadful things that were going to happen at the antenatal class this time. *Looking forward to it* was a long way from the truth.

That evening, as she climbed into Ben's car, her stomach was churning, and not because the baby was refusing to move off of her bladder. "I just don't understand the competitiveness," Holly said as they drove away from Bourton. "Everything is a competition. I swear if there was a prize for the biggest placenta these women would do a video call just to show everyone the size of theirs. "

"They're not that bad."

"They are," Holly insisted. When one woman had mentioned how she nearly wet herself when she was playing leapfrog with her niece, Clarissa mentioned how she had done a 5k park run that weekend. She boasted how her pelvic floor had held out perfectly even after a chia seed internal wash. What the hell was that? When another said how they'd got a new car ready for all the bags, car seats and pram paraphernalia, another got on the NCAP site to explain why the car they had bought was infinitely better.

"We're not staying for the coffee and biscuits afterwards," Holly said, pre-empting the chance Ben might be persuaded into helping at the end.

"I thought you brought some fudge and things for people?"

"Exactly. I brought it so I don't have to stay. Supplying the treats is my good will gesture. And my reward is getting out of there before they start talking about how long they are doing their perineal massages for." Even Ben had to shudder at that one. There were some things you just didn't want to discuss with other people, and she was fairly sure that all of those subjects had been brought up in this class at some point.

"You know, it wouldn't hurt you to get to know some of them a little better. You're going to want some mummy friends."

"I've got mum friends. I've got Caroline."

"I mean new mummy friends. You know the type like you who don't know what they're doing." A sudden look of horror flashed on Ben's face at the realisation of how horrendous his words had sounded. "I meant us. I meant that neither of us really knows what we're doing. Together. No, no! Not that we don't know what we're doing together. I mean, together with the baby."

"Do you want me to give you a spade there?" Holly asked, watching Ben's face flush redder and redder as he tried to dig himself out of his hole.

Finally, after an extended pause before he tried again.

"I just meant other mums you and the baby could hang out with."

"I understand what you're saying. I do. But the parents at the group are nothing like me at all. Cath and Jenny are both taking a year off when their baby comes. Together. They are going to be at home for the first year after the baby's birth. Clarissa is an internet influencer, so she's just going to drag her baby along with whatever it is she does. Dawn is the only one who's actually got to go back to work fairly soon after the baby is born. Besides you're doing as much childcare as me. Maybe you should try to find some daddy friends to hang out with. You don't have any either."

A deep feeling of satisfaction rolled through Holly as Ben blanched white. Unfortunately, she didn't have time to bask in the glory for long. They were already there.

CHAPTER EIGHT

There were plenty of antenatal classes closer than Cold Aston, but Jess had insisted this was the best one. And as she was paying for it, they couldn't really refuse. Besides, a lot of the classes that ran in Bourton and Stow were in the daytime, or in the early evening, when Ben couldn't always be certain that he would be home in time. Not with some of the clients he was working for now. Work dinners and extended lunches were now a much bigger feature of his life, but the weekends tended to be fairly protected, even though he should probably have spent the time getting an early night. It was a far cry from just working at the village branch. At times, she couldn't help but feel guilty about how hard he was working so they could have flexibility when the baby came, particularly when he didn't get home until gone ten some nights, bleary-eyed, barely finding enough energy to have a shower and eat some dinner before he dragged himself up to bed.

The luxury multi-purpose hall was on the edge of the complex, and had already been set out with a circle of large blue cushions on the floor. The circle of doom, Holly like to think of it, in which they all sat, facing the centre so they could desperately try to avoid eye contact while watching each other squirm with varying amounts of embarrassment as Florence, the instructor and former midwife, talked about their vulvas opening like a flower, and showed different techniques to avoid tearing. This set up, Holly decided, also allowed Florence to have her first chuckle of the evening as she observed all the heavily pregnant women struggling to get to the ground. And then another good giggle at the end when they had to get back up again. No, Holly wasn't bitter about her situation at all.

Thankfully, she was one of the first there, meaning she could drop off her fudge next to the water cooler, then get Ben to help her to the ground before there weren't too many people to watch her trying to shift her centre of gravity.

"Right, talk to me intently," Holly said, locking her eyes on Ben as she attempted to adjust the pillow beneath her so it didn't feel like a small baby elephant was stamping down on her pelvis. She should have gone to the toilet before she sat down, she thought. Well, it was too late now. She wasn't standing up again unless she really had to.

"Talk to you?" Ben asked. "About what?"

"Anything. People won't strike up a conversation with us if we're having a really important conversation when they come in. Haven't you noticed that?"

"No. I can't say I've paid that much attention to it."

"Well, I have. Now talk to me."

"About what?"

"About anything. I don't mind."

Ben pressed his lips momentarily together before an idea visibly clicked within him.

"Jamie and Caroline mentioned a baby shower again last week?" Ben said. Immediately, Holly's face hardened.

"What did you tell them?"

"That you weren't that keen on it, but maybe you could do something small with just the three of you and perhaps your mum and Drey."

While Ben's answer sounded fairly reasonable, a low growl resonated from Holly's throat. "Why did you tell them that? You know Jamie can't do small. She'll want to invite the people from the care home. And then your sister. We'll have to invite her because she's paying for all this. And then Mum will want to invite Aunty Janet if it's a big event and it'll be a full on baby shower before you know it."

"And that's a bad thing, why?"

It was Holly's turn to chew the question over and figure out something to say. She had always enjoyed baby showers, although she tended to buy whatever soft toy she fancied, rather than anything on the parents' wish list. Inevitably those lists were of things which were either absurdly expensive, or utterly unsentimental, like a bin with a twisty top to keep the stenches sealed away, or a microwave steriliser. But cost and gifts weren't where she had the issue. The issue was with Ben. Not that she'd ever tell him that.

Back in a former relationship, Ben had already lost one baby, and although it was very early on, Holly couldn't help but worry about how he would cope if it happened again. How they both would cope. She wasn't an only child out of choice; her mum and dad had lost several babies during their time together, and Holly took nothing for granted. That was why she'd delayed buying the cot for as long as she had, and only just let Ben paint the nursery. Should something happen to the baby, the fewer memories in the house, the better. That was her thinking, at least. And even though she never explained this to Ben explicitly, he knew exactly what the issue was.

"Holly, let's look at this objectively. You're in the third trimester. The scans have been positive. The baby's heart rate and weight have all been spot on in the fiftieth percentile. You have had no abnormal symptoms. I'm not worried. You should be at the stage where you're enjoying it now. Relaxing and making the most of these moments." As sweet as it was for him to say that, it was hard for her to believe him, knowing full well he had a checklist of all the possible things that could go wrong and the probability of them happening.

"If you can tell me how to make the most of water retention, I'd love to hear it," she said grumpily, but Ben responded by pulling her in closer to him.

"You don't need to worry. I've got you. I promise."

With her head against his chest, Holly closed her eyes and breathed in his scent. Moments like this, she felt so safe around Ben, like he would protect her no matter what was going on around her. She was lucky to have that. Yet no sooner had the thought formed than Giles' face flicked into mind. Giles and his oddly charming arrogance. And the way he made her laugh. Holly shook her head and scrunched her eyes shut, trying to remove that last thought from her mind. It was probably hormones, that was all. There was nothing between her and Giles. Nothing at all. And that was how she wanted things to stay. Needing more than just an internal dialogue to halt her runaway thoughts, she tilted her head up so that her lips found Ben's and kissed him more deeply than she had done all day.

"I love you," she said quietly as they broke apart.

"I love you, too," he whispered, then kissed her again.

"Oh wow, aren't you two the cutest of couples? Floyd, don't you think they're the cutest couple? I think they're the sweetest. It must be all the sugar they eat, right? Get it? Sweet? Because you have a sweet shop." The woman standing over Holly must have been three or four years younger, but she had the cackling laugh of someone in their seventies. Her hair was dyed blonde and, as always, styled impeccably. This time into perfect ringlets that fell in front of her shoulders. Thicker hair was one of the few good things about pregnancy Holly had discovered, but there was no way Clarissa's hair was all her own. It had to be extensions of some sort, but she could never bring herself to ask. Clarissa was the type of woman who wore sunglasses on the top of her head, regardless of whether it was actually summer or not, and whose lipstick didn't smudge regardless of how many sips of her water bottle she took. On top of that, despite being the same number of weeks along as Holly, she could also drop to the ground and stand back up again without the need of a crane—or at least an extra pair of hands—to help her, and had the uncanny ability of making Holly feel an inferior parent in every way possible.

"Clarissa," Holly shifted slightly away from Ben.

"Floyd," Ben reached out a hand to Clarissa's husband, who grunted a greeting as he shook it once, then dropped it hastily.

"So how's your week been?" Clarissa said, executing perfect posture as she dropped on the cushion next to Holly. "Any exciting news?"

"Nothing exciting. Just work."

"Oh." The sound came out from her lips like a gust of wind. As if mentioning the word, *work*, was about as toxic in this environment as sushi or soft cheese. "I don't know how you do it. I really don't. On your feet all day. It must be so tough. I really admire shop workers like yourself."

Holly didn't need to see Ben's face to know he was having the exact same reaction as she was. She could feel his hands clamping tighter around her waist.

"Holly is the owner, so she does get to take time off."

"Oh, of course. Of course, I didn't mean to offend you. I was just saying how much I admired your stamina, that's all. Honestly, three yoga classes and one prenatal massage a week and I'm worn out, aren't I, Floyd? Tell them how exhausted I am after my yoga lessons, Floyd. Go on tell them."

"Oh, she's exhausted," Floyd said rubbing his wife's shoulders, like just the thought of attending a class had caused her muscles to seize. From what Holly had seen of Floyd, he was a nice guy, although he very much adhered to the *don't speak until spoken to, a* rule clearly implemented by Clarissa.

"That's enough, Floyd," Clarissa said, cutting him off. "Thankfully, my followers are so supportive."

Fortunately, it didn't take long before the others arrived at the class and Clarissa found someone else in need of her attention and shortly after that, Florence started the class.

Holly settled back into Ben's arms. There were some videos, and chatting and one point where they passed around pumpkins with googly eyes stuck on and their mouths cut out into large, Os to show how wide their cervixes would go during labour, at which point, Holly preferred not to look.

The hour went by surprisingly quickly, and as the session drew to a close, Ben hoisted Holly up off the ground. Being true to his word, he thankfully didn't get pulled into any of the after session chat, and they headed promptly out into the chilled evening air together.

"There, that wasn't so bad, was it?" he said, his arms round her waist. "I mean, I never knew that you could squeeze a ping-pong ball out of a balloon like that. I think that might be my new party trick."

"You're only saying that because you don't have to squeeze anything out of your cervix. That last pumpkin…" She stopped and shuddered. "Anyway, I don't suppose there's any chance that our baby's going to pop out and bounce along the floor like that ping-pong ball did."

"If our baby lands on any floor, the hospital will have a lot to answer for," Ben said, responding to Holly's comment. "Now, can I tempt you with a foot massage and the new Ryan Reynolds film?"

"You'd watch a Ryan Reynolds film for me?"

"I'd do anything for you," he said. "Haven't you learned that by now?"

They were standing by the passenger side door, but neither Holly nor Ben had moved to open it. Instead, they were kissing again and as they kissed, Holly found herself thinking about the last time they had kissed like this; more than just a peck on the lips of the forehead and decided she couldn't remember when that had been.

"What do you think about missing the film and heading straight up to bed when we get in?" Ben said, his sentence disjointed by kisses.

"You want me like this?"

"Absolutely," Ben said, pulling her closer to him. She could feel her heart speeding up. Her breath growing shallower with every kiss. This was what they had been missing these last couple of months. There wasn't anything wrong with them at all, she told herself. The spark was still there.

"Okay," she whispered. "That sounds good."

"Great." When Ben broke away, he was grinning from ear to ear. "I think I'm going to have to put my foot down. Hold on."

True to his word, they were driving back to Bourton as close to the speed limit as Ben ever travelled. At one point he lifted Holly's hand to his lips and planted a soft, gentle kiss. As romantic as the moment could have been in coincided exactly with a large pothole in the road. The car lurched forward, resettling on the road again less that a second later.

A second which, for Holly, felt like an eternity.

"Ben..." she said, looking down at her lap and watching a dark patch spread out on the seat of her trousers.

"What is it?" he said, his eyes back on the road.

Holly struggled to find the words to her reply. Her heart was drumming in her chest, A sense of fear and disbelief causing her throat to close. She pulled in a long breath of air, fighting the dizziness that was now sweeping over her and finally managing to croak out a whispered sentence.

"My waters just broke."

CHAPTER NINE

Despite the inherently stressful nature of his job, there were very few times that Holly had seen Ben truly irate or panicked. There was of course their first introduction, where she had run out in front of his bike. He had certainly been left irate then, yelling at her in the middle of the road as she struggled to get up. There was also the time that he and Giles had come to blows at the beginning of her pregnancy. But mostly, Ben was an inherently calm man.

He had been calm when a massive storm nearly caused the roof of the sweet shop to fall in and he was forced to strip so he could plug the hole, despite not actually knowing Holly well at that point. He had even been relatively calm when she took him to a water park on their first date, even though he hadn't been able to swim. Either way, Holly had always assumed that Ben was the type of person who rose to stressful situations. It turns out that was not the case. At least, not when it came to Holly going into labour.

"Are you sure?" he said, panic causing his voice to hitch an octave higher than normal.

"Pretty sure," Holly said, looking down at the spreading dark patch in her lap.

Ben glanced down, following Holly's line of sight, only for the remaining colour to drain from his face. Gripping the steering wheel, he re-fixed his eyes on the road ahead.

"But we don't have the go bag. It's at the house. And it doesn't have any of the snacks in yet. I knew I should have put the snacks in already. Or nappies. I haven't even bought nappies yet. We hadn't even discussed if we are going to use disposable or reusable ones."

"Ben?" Holly snapped; her voice sharp enough to bring him his spiralling hysteria.

"You're right. We can buy snacks at hospital," he said, slipping back into his familiar pro-active voice. "Get out your phone. Open up the map app. We need to know which hospital is closer. Cheltenham or Cirencester. I checked last week and it was only one minute difference from home to each of the A&Es but, now they've put up temporary traffic lights just past Chedworth, I think Cheltenham may be a better call. Assuming the road is closed for some kind of festival. I should have checked for festivals. Cheltenham has festivals, doesn't it. No it's races they have. What if the races are on?"

"I don't think the races are this time of year," Holly said, comfortingly. "And especially not at this time of day. Horses can't run in the dark."

Somehow Ben's rapid ascent into terror was mildly comforting to Holly. A small swarm of butterflies has just landed in her abdomen, but other than that, she was doing a good job of keeping her nerves in check, although that she was getting nervous about the impending contractions. Currently though there was no real pain at all. Other than the headache she was certain was going to strike if Ben didn't stop soon.

"You're right, so you're saying we should go to Cheltenham?" he continued. "Is that what you're saying? Because if that's what you're saying then I should really turn around."

Unable to give him an answer, Holly pressed her hand against her rounded belly and tried to steady her thoughts. A moment later, she spoke again.

"I thought the contractions were supposed to come first?" she said, recalling how in antenatal class they had discussed how it never happens the way it does in the movies. Then again, Florence had suggested they avoid all movies for advice on childbirth. She practically forbade them watching any scenes that involved screaming in labour. According to Florence a *negative mindset* was the worst thing to take into the labour ward. Pushing aside the distracting thoughts, Holly focused on their current dilemma. Her hands had been resting on her belly for quite some time now, and other than a couple twists and turns and kicks to the kidneys, there hadn't been much going on.

"I don't know if I've had any contractions," she said again. "My stomach was hurting earlier but I thought that was gas." The comment sounded ridiculous now she said it out loud, but she had been struggling with terrible wind during the pregnancy and today's bout didn't seem particularly worse than any of the others she'd suffered.

"It could be a pre-labour membrane rupture," Ben said, now so pale he was near translucent. "That's what it's called when your water breaks early. They might have to induce. Not that that should be an issue. Given your waters have already broken they'll probably give you oxytocin. Or a balloon catheter. The odds of that working are good though it does depend on the condition of your cervix."

"Ben. Please stop. You're not making things better." That was a mild understatement. However bad labour was going to be, she doubted it would be much worse than listening to Ben saying cervix again. He shot her an apologetic look.

"Sorry, it's just… this is it. I thought I'd be a bit more prepared. I thought we had longer. But it will be fine. The statistics this late on are good."

"Ben…" she warned again. There were many times that Holly was grateful Ben read of all the scary pregnancy books, but, this was not one of them. With a deep breath Holly fought against the tirade of Ben's anxiety and her own. "Let's think about this logically. What's the first thing we are meant to do?" she asked, voicing her thoughts out loud, mostly to stop Ben talking.

"Ring the midwife," Ben replied to her question automatically. "The first thing you are meant to do is ring the midwife."

"Okay, in that case, let's do that. And maybe you should pullover. At least until we know where we're going."

Thankfully, Ben offered no objection as he steered the car into a nearby farm track and switched on the hazard warning lights.

"You're right, we just need to breathe,' he said, letting out a long puff of air. "Just breathe."

While Ben practiced the breathing exercise they had worked on that night. Holly picked up her phone and called the midwife. Her pulse kicked up a notch as she waited for her to pick up. She would need to ring her mum and dad when she was admitted, Holly considered the nerves creeping higher and higher. They'd be furious if she didn't. And then she'd need to ring Caroline, to let her know she wouldn't be able to work at the shop tomorrow. Then again, maybe her dad would be able to open if he is feeling up to it. A moment later the call went to voice mail. The same happened the second time, and the third.

"She's not picking up," Holly said.

"What do we do?" Ben said, the hitch in his voice back again. "Hospital?"

With both hands back on her stomach, Holly was struck by a sudden thought. A thought that made completely an utter sense.

"We should go back to the class. The gym. You know what it's like at the end of the session, someone will still be chewing Florence's ear off. She won't have left yet."

Ben pressed his lips tightly together obviously not convinced by this idea. "I don't know. I think hospital might be the best call."

"It's literally on the way, we'll pull up and if she's not there we head to Cheltenham. Let's go to Florence. I'll feel better if I speak to her first."

As Holly said the words, she realised how true it was. As much as she sometimes ridiculed the activities they did in these classes, Florence did seem to know what she was talking about. A few minutes pep talk—and a quick reminder of those breathing techniques that Holly hadn't really paid that much attention to—would put her mind at ease.

"Fine," Ben said, starting the car and performing a U-turn back up the road. "But you're staying in the car. I don't want you moving anywhere unnecessarily. Not when our baby is on its way."

"Our baby is on its way," Holly muttered, almost inaudibly.

CHAPTER TEN

As Holly, and Ben parked up in the exact same parking spot they had left only ten minutes earlier, Florence was leaving the hall, a large bag slung over her arms and Clarissa at her side.

"Oh God," Holly, muttered.

The last person she wanted to know she'd gone into labour was Clarissa. If she didn't hand out a hundred titbits of unsolicited advice, she would be asking for text message updates so that she could add them to her newsfeed, possibly with a picture of her posing with her placenta to boot.

Holly slunk down in her seat, the nerves that had been burgeoning had now hit a new high and it had nothing to do with the upcoming labour. Perhaps going to the hospital straight away was the right call after all.

"Just, be calm," she said to Ben as he unclipped his belt. "I only want Florence. Make it seem like we forgot something. Okay? Okay? Don't let Clarissa know what's going on."

Given the way Ben had swung open his car door without so

much as a peck on the cheek, Holly knew he hadn't been listening to her; he was barely out of the car before he broke into a sprint.

"Florence!" he waved his hands despite the fact the antenatal instructor was less than ten metres in front of him. "Holly's waters broke. The baby is on the way. What should we do? The baby's coming!"

Groaning, Holly covered her face with her hands and sank even lower. Within seconds her door was open and she was surrounded.

"Well, this is certainly unexpected, but that's not to worry," Florence said as she knelt on the ground. "Thirty-five weeks is early, but not so much we need to be concerned. Now tell me have you been timing your contractions?"

Despite hearing Florence's question, Holly's attention was elsewhere, stolen by Clarissa who was currently leaning in over Florence's shoulder, with her phone out.

"Do you mind? I could just do with a little bit of space," Holly said, fanning herself from the ever-growing heat that was flooding her cheeks.

"Of course," Clarissa said, stepping back. "Here, hold onto me. I suspect a bit of fresh air will do you the world of good. You know there's a trend in the States a few years ago where women were actually choosing to give birth outside in nature. That's not something I'd do personally. I mean, what about cleaning the baby afterwards? But still, there is something very calming about being outside. Taking in the fresh air before the magical moment arrives. And there's much better light out here too. You know, for some pictures of their first moments.

Holly gritted her teeth, the spasm that was flashing through her the closest thing to a contraction she had felt all evening.

"That's not the kind of space I meant," Holly hissed.

Ben was busy pacing and trying the midwife for the tenth time, Florence, thankfully, understood what Holly was trying to get across.

"I think I've got it from here, thank you," Florence said, standing up and facing Clarissa. "I think Floyd is still waiting in the car for you. You don't want to keep it running any longer than necessary. You know, with the impact on the environment and everything."

Clarissa opened her mouth in a similar fashion to a gawping fish, before closing it again, and twisting her lips into a tight pout.

"Of course. Of course. I should get going anyway. I left a lamb shank in the slow cooker. You know how dry they can get if you overcook them." Leaning forward very slightly she air-kissed Holly on both cheeks. "Mwah, mwah. I want to know everything. Keep us up to date, won't you Mama Bear? Send photos. And don't forget to record the crowning. Good luck!"

She offered a fluttering wave and high cheek-boned smile, before tottering off to where Floyd was indeed keeping the car running. Only when the car drove out of view did Holly allow herself to breathe out a sigh of relief.

"Right," Florence said, her voice almost ethereally soothing. "Now that it's a little less crowded, we can get back to the task in hand. Have you been timing your contractions? I take it they only started recently, or you were doing a very good job of keeping it under control in the class."

Holly shook her head. Being with Florence like this, suddenly made it feel all the more real. She was about to have a baby. Closing her eyes she pulled in a long breath before she spoke.

"No, the contractions haven't kicked in yet. Or at least, I don't think so, Ben said he thinks it might be… What did you say you thought it was? A pre-labour—"

"A pre-labour membrane rupture," Ben called over Florence's shoulder. "It's when the waters break early."

"Thank you Ben," Florence replied, with a tight-lipped smile. "And can you tell me when it happened exactly? You were in the car?"

"We'd just left here," Holly said, starting to speak before Ben could say anything else. "We were driving and the car hit a pothole."

"I should have been more careful, I should have been watching the road," Ben started again, but Florence put up a hand to silence him, before inhaling deeply through her nose.

"Okay, so the first thing I need to do is have a look at you, which isn't going to be possible in the car. Do you think you'll be okay to walk by yourself back into the hall?"

Holly didn't manage to get a reply out before Ben was answering for her.

"It's fine. I can support her."

"Actually, I'd like Holly to walk by herself. And perhaps you'd like to wait here, Ben. Just give Holly a little bit of breathing space while I take a quick look at what's going on. It's not the most magical part of the experience," she added.

Given how involved Ben needed to be with everything, Holly expected him to protest Florence's request. Thankfully she knew the exact way to mollify his concern.

"Florence is the expert in this, remember," she said, taking Florence's hand as she climbed out of her seat. "She's a former midwife. She's seen this a hundred times. It's probably best we do what she says."

With a pout of toddler proportions, Ben nodded his head.

"Okay, but it I'm going to help you walk to the door."

"Florence wants me to walk by myself, remember?" At this, Ben folded his arms across his chest and took a step back away from the car.

"I guess I'll just keep trying the midwife."

"Don't worry," Florence said. "She'll be in perfectly safe hands. And I'll call you immediately if I need you."

With a mixture of both trepidation and relief Holly kissed Ben on the cheek before waddling towards the main doors to the building.

Even as they approached the hall, Holly could feel Ben's eyes boring into her and a flutter of guilt joined the butterflies. She knew how Ben wanted to be involved in every single step, but she was grateful Florence had insisted he stayed behind. There was only so many facts and statistics you could hear about childbirth and labour.

"Okay," Florence said as they stepped inside. "How are you feeling?"

"Fine. Still just the same if I'm honest with you."

"Good. Now, I'm afraid I'm going to have to get a bit personal here Holly. Are you wearing pads. You know, to protect yourself from leakages?"

Leakages. That was a nice way to put it. Oh the glamour of pregnancy, Holly thought as she attempting to hide her humiliation at the question. All the magazines that promised glossy hair and radiant skin seemed to neglect these conversations. Along with a whole heap of other things too.

"Umm, yes. A friend suggested it to me, you know. Just in case. Although I've never really had any need for them." God, she wished the ground would swallow her right up. Was this really what life had become? These kinds of discussions with a woman she barely knew. Though surprisingly, her answer elicited a smile from Florence.

"Fantastic, if we can just head to the toilet and you can take that out and we can have a look. Don't worry, I've got gloves."

CHAPTER ELEVEN

"Drive," Holly said as she slammed the car door shut and buckled up her seat belt, having waddled from the hall so fast Ben hadn't even had a chance to get out of the car before she had jumped in it. "Drive now."

"What happened? Where's Florence?" Ben fumbled for his seat belt. "Where are we going? Cheltenham? We'll go to Cheltenham. Right."

Gripping her hands so hard she could feel her nails in her palms, Holly attempting to alleviate the burning that was still ongoing in her cheeks. Although it made no difference. No, she would probably remain red-faced for her entire life. Her voice cracked in her throat, before she spoke again.

"We're going home," she said. Ben turned to her wide-eyed.

"Okay, for how long? Did Florence say how long we should stay at home. Until the contractions are closer together? Has she rung ahead to the hospital? What about induction? Did she not say anything about that?"

It didn't matter how much she wished there was a way out

of it, there wasn't. Holly was going to have to say it. She was going to have to tell him.

"My waters didn't break, Ben. I'm not in labour."

"But I saw it. I saw your jeans… ohh."

Holly nodded and looked down at her lap. On the plus side, Florence had a spare pair of stretchy yoga pants in her bag, so at least Holly was wearing clean, dry clothes. But that was the only good news.

"The scientific name for it is Enuresis," she said, parroting the word Florence had so kindly used with her, before explaining what that meant.

"Enuresis," Ben repeated. "But it still means… it's just—"

"Yes, I wet myself. Yup. The bloody pothole caused me to wet myself."

"Oh."

Silence filled the car. She didn't want to look at Ben. She couldn't. After all, surely she should have been able to tell the difference between peeing herself and going into labour? But apparently not. As she could have predicted, Florence had been lovely about the whole episode, telling Holly she'd known dozens of women think the exact same thing, many of whom went straight to hospital. Holly wasn't sure if she was lying or not, but a least she hadn't gone all the way to A&E and taken up the time of some busy doctor just to be told she had no control over her bladder.

"Are you going to say something?" she said, unable to take the silence any longer. Anything would have been better than silence. Even Ben reciting off a hundred different statistics about incontinence. Though when she looked to Ben, she quickly discovered the reason for his lack of response.

His entire body was shaking as he gripped the steering

wheel. His jaw clenched so tightly together his lips had disappeared entirely and silent tears ran down his cheeks.

"Ben?"

The moment his eyes met hers, he erupted. Laughter shattering the quiet around them.

"Oh Holly," he sniffed as he attempted to wipe away the tears.

"This is not funny." Holly said, thumping him lightly on the arm.

"It is. It is very funny."

"It is mortifying. You can't tell anyone. I mean that. Not Caroline, or Jamie, or anyone."

"But it's such a good story," he said between heavy gulps of air, wheezing as he struggled to get his laughter under control.

"This is not a good story. It's utterly humiliating. Oh my god, what if Florence brings it up in our next class? And Clarissa. She thinks I've gone into labour. She saw me. She wants photos."

At this Ben dropped his head onto the steering wheel, tears trickling down his face. Holly on the other hand, was having a hard time seeing the funny side of the situation.

"This is horrendous. I'm never going there again. I can't. I can't."

She dropped her head into her hands and tried to ignore the fact that Ben was still chuckling beside her. If he didn't stop laughing soon she'd get out and walk. Or at least threaten to. She wasn't going to actually walk, but the last thing she needed was Ben adding to her embarrassment.

"We just need to treat it as a lesson," Ben said, when he had finally stemmed his laughter enough that he could talk properly again. "For starters, I am going to put the snacks in the go bag tonight. And should we have more than one? We should keep one in the car in case we're travelling. And it might be a good idea to have one in the sweetshop too. I'll make them up tonight."

For a second Holly considered mentioning that she didn't think she had enough nightdresses for all Ben's planned go bags, but she was just grateful, he was talking about something other than her incontinence.

"If anyone's to blame for this, you know it's you," she said as he pulled out of the car park. "I don't hit potholes when I'm driving on my own."

Ben let out a chuckle that was slightly more with Holly than at her.

"In that case," he said, reaching across and taking her hand. "Would I be able to tell Caroline and Jamie? Given that's it's my fault and everything?"

Holly went to pull her hand out of his grip but he held on tight, pulling it towards him and kissing her gently on the knuckles.

"How about, when we get in, I give you a foot massage?"

"And my back too?" Holly added, determined to get all she could out of this deal.

"And perhaps quarter of a glass of rosé," Ben added.

"Well now you're talking," Holly replied. This time, it was she who kissed Ben's knuckles, before their hands fell on top of the gear stick, fingers entwined.

Her hand was in such a position when her phone rang. Unfortunately her bag was now in the footwell, which had become more and more difficult to reach with every passing week. It took several manoeuvres before she managed to grab it.

"I'm sure it'll just be Mum," Holly said. "And you can't say anything to her, either. No one is to know about tonight, you understand."

"Even after the baby is born?"

After shooting Ben a glare which she assumed conveyed her answer perfectly, Holly glanced down at her phone, and frowned. It was a London number on the screen, although it wasn't one she recognised. Her initial thought was that perhaps it was Dan, her ex. He had, she assumed, returned to London after she turned down his proposal last year, but then he would ring from a mobile number, wouldn't he? And why would he ring her at all? She pulled her hand out of Ben's grip and stared at the phone.

"Everything alright?" Ben asked.

Holly couldn't explain it. A feeling of nervousness was tingling through her. "I don't know," she said. But she had to answer the phone. She knew that much.

A small echoey voice came out of the speaker the moment Holly answered. Like whoever was calling her was speaking in a very empty room.

"Holly?"

"Drey? Drey, is that you? Where are you? Is something wrong?" Holly responded.

A slight pause hovered in the air, followed by the sharp intake of breath.

"Is there any chance that you or Ben have the number of a lawyer in London?"

CHAPTER TWELVE

Holly stared at the car clock, only to check the time again against her phone, and her watch discovering they were all exactly the same.

"It's fine," Ben said, reaching across and squeezing her knee. "She'll be fine."

"What the hell was she doing? Arrested. In London. I should ring her father. I should definitely ring her father." Her foot was tapping against the footwell of the car. And to make her even more uncomfortable, the extra adrenaline in her bloodstream had the baby twisting and turning like it was auditioning for Cirque de Soleil.

"Do you want to ring her father? I'm not saying I disagree, but isn't that exactly what Drey asked you *not* to do?"

"So you don't think I should ring him?"

Holly had been feeling physically nauseous from the second Drey had hung up the phone. Drey, her uber responsible Saturday girl, whom she trusted more than many people double her age, had been arrested in London. And needed a lawyer.

"This man. This Elliot, are you sure he's good?" Holly asked Ben for what had to be the tenth time.

"He's good. He'll be able to handle this."

Thank goodness Ben was with her. That was the thought that had gone through Holly's head half a dozen times or more because she wouldn't have had a clue where to start finding a lawyer. Thankfully, Ben had house shared with a law student during his university years, and the pair were still in touch. Even more thankfully, Elliot had graduated and gone on to become a very successful lawyer *and* he still lived in London.

"What would you do?" Holly said, her mind flitting around faster than she could keep track of. "Do you think I should ring Drey's father? Do you think I should let him know?"

At this point, Holly had expected Ben to give her a definitive, *yes*. He was as straight down the line as they came. And family was hugely important to him, so his hesitance took her by surprise.

"She's eighteen, isn't she?"

"So? Is that important?"

"Yes, it is important. Drey's an adult. She could have rung her dad if she wanted to. I'm guessing she doesn't want him to know. She didn't even want us to go up and get her."

"Like we could just leave her there."

Holly dropped her head into her hands and let out an exasperated groan. Her body was fraught with tension. Her hands clenched so tightly, her knuckles were white and she could feel her molars grinding together.

"You need to stay calm," Ben said, moving his hand from her leg to do a sweep across her belly. "You need to think of this one. Getting stressed isn't going to help."

"Well, I can't stay calm. Not when it's all I can think about. Talk to me about something different. Tell me about work?"

"My work? You hate hearing about my work."

"Can you just talk to me!" Holly's voice came out far louder than she had expected to. "Sorry, just tell me something. What trips do you have planned for next week? Any interesting new clients?"

"One or two actually," Ben said. "And I'm probably going to need to stay over on the Friday night too."

"On a Friday night?" This piece of news was the first thing that actually distracted Holly. "Why will you have to be there, then? You're normally free on the weekend."

"I know. But it's the particular client. Apparently, he likes the whole wining and dining thing."

"That could be fun."

"I doubt it," Ben said. A ripple of tension seeped into the car. They had spent a fair amount of time in the counselling sessions discussing how Ben was feeling with the added pressures of the promotion and how he was going to balance that with the baby when it came. As such, Holly knew it was an area she needed to tread carefully around and right now was probably not the right time to discuss it. Still, she needed to keep her mind off Drey, rotting away in a jail cell filled with unsavoury characters and brash, cruel police officers. Thankfully, another topic sprang to mind.

"You know, we still haven't discussed names properly," she said with a newfound spark.

"You want to discuss names? Now?" Ben said. Outside, the sulphur yellow streetlights emitted a hazy glow that snaked along the motorway ahead of them. London was feeling impossibly far away today.

"Well, I guess it is sensible to start at least thinking about names before the baby arrives," Holly pressed. "You know what they said at the class. Only four percent of first-borns actually arrive on their due date."

"Okay, so what do you have in mind? Do you want to do boys or girls names first?"

"I don't mind. Why don't you tell me any names you have in mind?"

Ben chewed down on his bottom lip, his eyes fixed on the road in front of him. "I'm not sure. I was thinking maybe Christopher for a boy."

"Christopher?" Holly said, aghast. "Do you not remember Christopher Petty at school?"

"Christopher Petty?"

"He was the one who got busted for selling cigarettes to the Year Sevens, then when they cleared out his locker they found half a bottle of lighter fuel in there, along with loads of really weird drawings of knives and bird skulls and things."

"So Christopher is a no, then?"

"Christopher is a no."

"Okay, how about Alan?"

"Alan. It's a bit old, isn't it?"

"What about Stephen?" Holly wrinkled her nose. She couldn't help it, it was just Ben's suggestions were completely off the mark. "Okay, then," Ben said with a hint of acridity. "What did you have in mind? You make suggestions."

Puffing out her cheeks, Holly exhaled a large breath of air. She thought about names in passing, occasionally homing in on one or two. But mostly, like the baby shower, she had considered it tempting fate to get her heart too set on anything.

"Actually," she said. "There is one name I like. If it's a girl."

"Okay, what's that?"

"Agnes," she said. "If they're a little girl, then I think I'd like to call her Agnes. In fact, I really want to call her that, at least her middle name, if it's not her first."

She turned and looked to Ben, expecting him to offer her the same sort of response she had done to his suggestions, but instead, a soft smile stretched on his lips, and as he glanced at Holly, she felt a warm tingle spread within her.

"Agnes sounds perfect," Ben said. "I like it. Agnes Thornbury."

"That sounds good."

Holly placed her hand on top of his on the steering wheel. The tension that had gripped her body only moments ago had dissipated, dissolved into the air.

Twenty minutes later, they were off the motorway and repeatedly stopping and starting at the traffic lights that littered London's roadways. The tension returned in force.

"Okay," said Ben, as they approach an imposing grey stone building. "This is where she said she was. Do you want me to come in with you?"

Holly looked at the front doors to the station. Prior to moving to Bourton, her experience with the police had been extremely limited. However, due to Giles' previously unscrupulous schemes, she had become more acclimatised to them. Still, the largest station she'd had to go to then was Cheltenham and at the time she'd thought that was massive. This station, however, with its dozen police cars parked out the front, was an entirely different experience. "I'll be fine," Holly said, hoping she sounded more confident than she felt. "You find somewhere to park the car. I'll ring you when I've got her."

Ben nodded in agreement, although neither of them looked entirely convinced as Holly stepped outside and felt the clammy evening air of September in London sticking to her skin.

"Oh Drey, what have you got yourself into?"

CHAPTER THIRTEEN

Holly's fingers were drumming on the dashboard as she stared at the brightly lit entrance to the police station.

"Shouldn't you have heard from Elliot by now?" She said to Ben, for probably the tenth time in as many minutes. "You said he thought it was all straightforward. That he didn't think they'd charge her."

"I don't know any more than you," Ben said. "I don't have much experience on getting bailed out of jail."

Holly let out a long hiss. She should just stay quiet and wait, she knew. After all, there was nothing else she could actually do, but silence caused the worst images of Drey to rise in her head, and she couldn't bear that. So before she could stop herself, she was talking again.

"And you're sure he has experience in this type of thing?" She started again. "Because the wrong type of lawyer could make the whole situation worse, couldn't it? I mean, if he doesn't know what he's doing, perhaps we should have called someone else. Got a second opinion."

"I don't think police stations work like that, Holly."

"But you don't know, do you?" She was just about to ask another question, when the doors to the police station open and out walked a well-dressed man with flaming red hair and a large black briefcase, although Holly paid him little attention, as beside him, in her all denim ensemble, was Drey.

It was probably the fastest Holly had moved in five months, as she leapt out of the car, and strode across the car park. The minute she reached Drey, she wrapped her arms around her in the tightest bear hug possible, before promptly letting her go and pushing her back out to arm's length.

"What the hell were you thinking?" she began.

"What are you doing here?" Drey responded. "I told you I could get a train back home."

"That is not an answer," Holly replied. She was about to say a lot more when Ben's hand appeared on her shoulder.

"I think we can talk about it on the way home, can't we?" He said, before he stepped past Holly and stretched out his hand. "Elliot, long time no see. Thank you for this. I hope you're keeping well."

The two men shook hands briefly before going in for a quick hug.

"It's been too long, mate. Far too long. Life treating you well?"

"You could say that," Ben said, with a nod toward Holly's belly. Elliot's eyes widened before he let out a whistle.

"Wow, congratulations."

"Thank you."

"You kept that quiet. You'll have to let me know when they come along. We could get together. Have a drink. Wet the baby's head."

"That sounds good," Ben said. "And thank you for tonight. I owe you."

"Don't mention it. I'm sure you'll be able to repay the favour with some banking advice in the future. Or just a couple more drinks. Though we need to stay off the Jager bombs. You'll remember what happened last time."

"I think you'll find I am much more mature than that now," Ben replied dryly, at which Elliot let out a hearty chuckle.

"It was only four years ago, mate. Though I guess that was nothing compared to the old days. Remember that Soho pub crawl?"

At this, Holly felt the men had forgotten the reason they were there altogether.

She glanced at Drey, who was rubbing her eyes, and Holly couldn't help but notice they were slightly red rimmed.

"What happens now?" she said, bringing the men back to the situation at hand. "Did you have to post bail? Is there a court date set?"

Elliot looked back at her, as if surprised she was still there. "No, there's none of that. The charges were entirely trumped up. She's got no priors, never been in any sort of trouble. There was no way they were going to stick, and they knew that."

"What does that mean?"

"It means we can get out of here," Drey said, suddenly more awake, although Holly grabbed her hand before she could have any ideas about disappearing.

"Is that true?" she checked with Elliot. "Can she go?"

"She can. They dropped everything. She's been let off with a caution, that's all."

All the tension that had been fixed in Holly's muscles for the last three hours dropped away. "Thank goodness for that."

She looked at Drey, waiting for some kind of response. Or perhaps even a smile, but got nothing.

"I guess we should get a move on, then," Ben said, reading the new level of tension that was tightening around them. "And thank you again, Elliot."

After several more thanks, this time from Drey and Holly, and a couple of awkward hugs, Holly, Ben and Drey headed back to the car. A light drizzle had set in and was misting the air, and it looked like it was going to be a long drive back. Though as the engine started, it was clear that all the worry that had been plaguing Holly on the way there was being replaced by adrenaline filled fury.

"You went to an illegal protest?" she snapped.

From the back seat, Drey huffed.

"Protesting is not illegal. We have the right to protest peacefully."

"This one obviously wasn't peaceful then."

A warbling hiss reverberated from Drey's lips. "It was fine. There was nothing wrong with it. It was all fine. It was… It was the… look, I didn't ask you to come and pick me up. I would have been fine."

In the front of the car, Ben shot Holly a look. Holly had always known Drey to be fiercely independent. It was one of the things that made her love her so dearly—and kept the shop going in the days with Maud—but this girl was nothing like the one that she chatted to for hours on end in the shop. She was stone cold. Not even so much as a thank you had passed her lips since they turned up. When she glanced in her rear-view mirror, Holly saw Drey's knees were bouncing up and down and her hands still quivering despite the fact she had clasped them together.

"Ben, can you stop the car, please?" Holly said.

"Sorry?"

"Just stop. Please stop the car."

After offering only the slightest glance, Ben hit the hazard warning lights and pulled over at the side of the road. The instant the car stopped, Holly pinged off her seat belt and immediately jumped into the back seat of the car.

"What are you doing?" Drey coughed out, but it was too late. Tears were already welling in her eyes and the tremble she had tried so hard to keep at bay was now causing her entire body to quake. Holly squeezed herself up next to her, slipping her arm around Drey's back, and pulled her into her shoulder. There was no resistance anymore. No avid objections, or insisting she was fine. Just heavy sobs racking through her body.

"He told me it was legal. He said the police never come to them, anyway. And I… I..."

"It's okay. It's okay." Holly brushed the younger woman's hair as Drey's head rolled on her shoulder. "You're fine. You're absolutely fine."

"I didn't think that could happen. I didn't think…" The words petered out again, though this time she didn't continue them. Holly fixed her seat belt and with a nod to Ben he restarted the engine and carried on out of London. Gradually the tears dried up, and the sobbing grew quieter and a little later, when a bump in the road caused her head to loll to the side, Holly saw for certain that Drey had fallen asleep on her.

"Is she?" Ben asked from the front.

"Yeah, she's out cold. She must be exhausted."

Holly gazed at the girl draped on her shoulder. Sometimes she looked so grown up with her hair and make-up done far more stylishly than Holly could ever manage. But at that moment, with smudged mascara, blotchy cheeks and her hair splayed out, she looked so very young.

"Do you think we should drop her at home?" Holly asked. "If we do, then her dad's going to want to know why she's not still away, like she is meant to be."

"So, do you want her to stay with us? I mean, I'm okay with that and everything, but thinking from a parental point of view, is that really the right thing to do?"

A heavy sigh escaped from Holly's lips. "I have no idea," she said. "I mean, yes, her dad should definitely know, but maybe there's a reason she didn't want him to know right now. She's really shaken up. If he's going to lay into her the moment she gets home, then that won't help things at all. Maybe we should take her to our place, then have a talk in the morning and decide where to go for there."

She lifted her weight onto her arms and tried to readjust her position so that there wasn't so much pressure on her back. At times like these, where it felt like her whole body had tripled in size, she wondered how on earth people having twins or triplets coped. Hopefully, they didn't have to take late-night trips to get teenagers out of jail.

Given how concerning Holly was finding the whole situation, it surprised her to see that Ben was smiling at her.

"What? What is it?" she said, feeling suddenly nervous at this. His smile was so broad it was bordering on insane.

"You said our place," Ben said, still unable to suppress his grin. "You said we should take her to our place."

"Did I? I mean… you always call it our place."

"I know I do. But you don't. You deliberately don't. But you did then."

Holly wasn't sure what her reaction was meant to be. Ben was right. She deliberately referred to it as his house because that's what it was. He bought it, and he paid the mortgage, and she wasn't even registered as an occupant there, but seeing his face one thing was certain, she liked that smile.

"Does that mean you might consider giving up your room at Jamie's?" he said hopefully. The niggling doubt immediately returned to the pit of Holly's belly.

"I think we've got enough on our plate to think about that now," she said with a gesture to Drey, still asleep on her. "But I'll think about it. Will that be okay?"

"Thinking about it would be great."

When they arrived back home, Drey dragged herself from the car and into the kitchen where Holly poured her a glass of water while Ben made up the sofa bed.

"Do you want to talk about it?" Holly said, sitting opposite her with a herbal tea in hand.

Drey shook her head.

"There's nothing to talk about. I was dating an arsehole. That's the long and short of it." Her voice started to crack, and Holly reached across the table to take her hand. "You won't tell Dad, will you? He'll be furious. He's said all along that Eddy was trouble. Please, don't tell him. I don't want him to know."

There was so much pain in Drey's eyes, and Holly desperately wanted to say she wouldn't, but what type of mother would that make her?

"We'll talk about it in the morning, okay? Right now, you need to sleep. But you are going to have to tell him. Whether or not you want to, honesty is always the best option."

At these words, Drey shook her head and laughed. "I hardly

think you're one to be giving lectures to me on honesty, now do you?"

It had come out as a flippant, throw away mark, yet despite her laughter, it didn't feel like a joke. A chill prickled Holly's skin.

"What's that supposed to mean?" she said. "What do you mean by me not giving lectures on honesty?"

Drey shifted backwards, a chewing motion rolling over her lips. "Forget I said it. Forget I said anything."

"Drey?"

"I'm just tired, that's all," she said, backing away out the room. "I'll speak to him. I'll speak to him soon. I promise."

But even as Drey polished off her water and headed to the bathroom, her words continued to linger in Holly's mind. It didn't sound like nothing. It didn't sound like nothing at all.

CHAPTER FOURTEEN

The next morning, Holly let Drey sleep in. It was, after all, a Sunday, and given how traumatic her Saturday night had been, she suspected she needed it. Holly then gave her own dad, Arthur, a quick ring to say that something had come up and he would need to open up the shop on his own.

Both she and Ben had agreed that having the two of them there for the conversation with Drey would most likely make it feel like an interrogation, and so Ben headed out for a run, leaving Holly to bake some breakfast banana muffins and wait for Drey to wake up. It was a fairly long wait.

At ten-fifteen, a bleary-eyed Drey dragged herself into the kitchen where sweet, freshly baked aromas wafted from the oven.

"Perfect timing," Holly said. "The muffins are just cool enough to eat. Do you want a cup of tea? I've just boiled the kettle."

Holly already knew from their time at the shop that Drey was not a morning person and was unsurprised when the teenager offered only a nod of response as she slunk into the chair. As Holly dropped two tea bags into mugs, she couldn't help but see the similarities between herself and her own mother, Wendy. Tea and cake were her solutions to almost every issue that arose in life and Holly had lost count of the number of times they would sit at the kitchen table with a cuppa and cake and put the world to rights. The amount of cake both Wendy and Arthur ate it was a miracle they were both in such good shape. Hopefully she and the baby inherited the same genes. As the kettle hissed loudly, Drey finally cleared her throat.

"You really didn't need to pick me up last night," she said.

"We were hardly going to leave you there. I'm just glad Elliot was able to get you out, and you weren't charged." Holly bit down on her tongue. It would be far too easy to go into a tirade about acting responsibly and what she would have done if Ben hadn't had a friend to help her out, but it didn't feel like a good place to the start the conversation. So instead she added a splash of milk to the two cups and carried them over to Drey. "I'm glad you called me. I'm glad you know you can always call me if you need to," Holly continued, softening her tone. "How are you feeling now? Are you ready to tell your dad about it? You know, I really think you should." Drey stared wordlessly at her mug. "Drey…" Holly spoke softly, as if trying to prise a toy from a toddler's grip. "You have to tell him about this."

A sharp scoff accompanied Drey's first sip of her tea. "Like he'll understand. He's already mad at me because my grades last year weren't as high as he thought they should be. And I know he thinks I focused more on the shop than my studies, but I didn't. I really didn't. Trust me, this would just add to the long list of reasons as to why he's disappointed in me."

"He's your father. He wants what's best for you, that's all. That's all any parent wants. I can be there when you talk to him if that would help?"

With another scoff and sip of her tea, Drey shook her head. "It's fine. I'll do it. I can do it. I just need to work out what I'm going to say, that's all."

Holly nodded. There were a couple more things she wanted to bring up, and thought it unlikely they get any better responses, but she needed to ask.

"What about Eddy? Have you heard from him?"

The snort that escaped Drey's lips told Holly everything she needed to know.

"Oh, I'm done with him. One hundred percent done. You know, he hasn't even called me. Even after I messaged him last night and said that the police had arrested me, he didn't message. I mean, what type of guy does that? What type of guy would leave his girlfriend like that?"

"The type of guy you do not need in your life," Holly replied. Remembering she had not yet got them anything to eat, she grabbed a banana muffin from the countertop and popped it onto a plate for Drey. Given that Drey's appetite was normally comparable to her own, the way she picked at the muffin tentatively told Holly that she was still a long way from feeling okay, but there was still another question Holly wanted to ask her. Or rather, needed to ask her.

"Last night," Holly said. "When we were in here, you said something about being honest. About me not knowing about honesty. What did you mean by that?"

Drey squirmed visibly as she abandoned the muffin altogether, dropping it back onto the plate.

"I wasn't thinking straight last night. I have no idea what I was talking about." Her words may have sounded convincing, but her eyes were down at the table, staring intently at the muffin and avoiding Holly's at all costs.

"I don't believe you," Holly said. "You can tell me what you meant."

Silence swelled between the pair. A nervousness dried Holly's mouth. It couldn't possibly be what she thought, could it? No, there was no way Drey could know that. "Drey, whatever you think it is I've done, I think I've got a right to know, don't you?" The words hovered in the air between them and for a moment Holly was convinced that Drey was going to brush the comment off again. But what she said instead was…

"I've seen you, doing your food shopping. I've seen you… with him. Laughing, chatting. And I've seen you there more than once."

"Oh."

"I'm not going to say anything to anyone," Drey added quickly.

"It's not what you think."

The pair spoke at the exact same time, then shrank away slightly, a mirror image of each other. It was Drey who repeated herself first.

"I'm not going to say anything. You know I'm not. You do whatever you think is right for you. I'll respect that. And it wasn't right of me to bring it up like that."

"No, you had every right to bring it up. But it's not… it's not…" Holly took a moment to compose herself. "We just have the same shopping schedule that's all."

Drey raised an eyebrow indicting exactly how weak her excuse was.

"Honestly. And yes, I enjoy Giles' company, as a friend, that's all. He makes me laugh. But, you know how much the others think of him."

"You mean they think he's a snake?" Drey said bluntly. "Because he *is* a snake."

"He *was* a snake," Holly said. "I know that, and I can't possibly expect you to understand, because I don't understand. He's just a grown man who's made a lot of mistakes and is trying to make right by some of them."

"Look," Drey said. That young girl, unsure of herself and afraid of her father, was gone and replaced with the mature young woman and friend that Holly spoke to week in and week out at the shop. "I just care about you. I don't care if you're seeing a hundred guys, as long as that's what makes you happy. I mean that. And I meant what I said about not saying anything. I wouldn't do that to you."

"Thank you. I know that, but really, there is nothing between Giles and me."

A slight pause filtered between the pair.

"About my dad," Drey said tentatively. "I'll promise I'll tell him. I just need to work out what I'm going to say."

"Well, aren't we a mess?" Holly laughed. As she caught Drey's eye, a small sad smile twisted on the corner of her lips.

"I'm eighteen. I'm supposed to be a mess. What's your excuse?"

Holly laughed sadly. She only wished she had one.

CHAPTER FIFTEEN

During the following days, Holly found herself feeling more and more awkward and uncomfortable. For starters, she was definitely running out of room in her abdomen. It was now almost impossible to find a comfortable position to sit or stand and it was a thousand times worse when it came to sleeping. Her body was on its own thermostat, which felt ten degrees higher than it was supposed to be, and lying down proved the exact cue her bump needed to start wiggling with maximum force. At one point, she genuinely wondered if it had fractured a rib.

"A wriggly baby is a strong baby," Caroline said to her at the shop on the Wednesday afternoon as they pottered around finding things to fill the quiet period. "That's a good thing."

"I want a strong baby. That's great and everything. I'd just rather it didn't use my kidneys as a punching bag."

"Oh, people with their first babies. Just you wait, this will all be old hat by the time you're on the second."

Holly shuddered visibly. "Trust me, I've got to get through

this one yet. And I don't think Ben and I are in quite the position to start thinking about another."

"Are you not? Michael and I were talking about how happy you two looked last night. You were really relaxed."

"I guess."

They'd had a couples' night at the pub the previous evening. Caroline and Michael, Jamie and Fin and her and Ben. It was a big change from when Holly had started to go to the pub with the group, but she had to admit that the transition felt easy. Caroline was right. The night had been filled with laughter, and Ben and Holly had sat close to each other the entire time, their hands resting on one another's knees. She had thought at the time how this would be absolutely fine. How her life panning out like this for the next twenty, thirty, forty years would be absolutely fine. But then she had thought about what Drey had said, about fine not being good enough, and she had started to wonder. Then again, what did Drey know? She was only a kid, only just experiencing her first proper break up. And she'd just got herself arrested at a protest. No, Drey was probably the worst person to be basing any decisions on.

"Earth to Holly?"

"Sorry?"

"Did you hear me? I said, is that your phone beeping upstairs?"

It still took Holly another minute to process what Caroline had said to her.

"My phone?"

"I just heard it beeping upstairs. Do you want me to get it? If you don't want to hobble up the stairs."

Holly was about to accept her offer when she realised exactly who it would be texting her. It was bad enough Drey knowing that she had been meeting Giles in secret; she didn't what Caroline to be put in the awkward position of knowing too.

"It's fine. It's probably just my phone provider messaging me to say I'm eligible for a free plan upgrade. I'll read it later."

"If you're sure?"

"I am. Now, we should probably sort out that bottom shelf of Jelly Tots and Nerds. I think they need tidying up."

And then, because Holly needed a distraction, she got to work straightening up the shelves.

After Drey's revelation on the Sunday morning, Holly had decided to go cold turkey on the Giles front and had ghosted him, as the young people called it. It probably wasn't the kindest or smartest, let alone most mature thing to do, but she knew the second she replied, she'd get drawn into a conversation and then she wouldn't be able to stop thinking about him until they met up again. The problem was, she wasn't really able to stop thinking about him now, either. And it didn't help that he had messaged every day. Nothing salacious or improper. Just every day checking up, hoping that she was okay and letting her know he was there if she needed anything. That was all. Which made it even harder.

"Are you okay?" Caroline said once again, jerking Holly out of her thoughts. "You've been staring at that same shelf for two minutes now."

"Pardon?"

"Right. That's it. You need to take a break. There is no need for us both to be here. Honestly. Go home. Watch some television or something."

"Honestly, I'm fine," Holly tried to insist, but at that moment the baby kicked so hard it caused her to gasp.

"Home, now. Did you bring the car, or do you need a lift?"

"I can walk. It'll probably help."

Caroline didn't look convinced, but she was obviously happy to concede this victory having already persuaded her boss to go home.

"Fine, walk. But text me when you get home, okay?"

Relieved that she didn't have to pretend to be on top form anymore, Holly headed upstairs and grabbed her coat and bag, although she didn't bother to check what her phone said. She would deal with that later. Or more likely, just keep ignoring it.

Outside, the air was filled with an annoying drizzle that dampened her clothes and hair, but didn't really warrant having an umbrella out. Across the road, she saw a woman pushing a pram with a plastic covering over the top to keep the baby dry. Did they have one of those? They had a sunscreen, and a mirror for the car, and had several breast pumps in her online basket but still hadn't decided which to buy. Caroline had passed on almost everything they needed to get started, but every time she saw a mother and baby, Holly was reminded of yet another thing they didn't possess and would no doubt need to purchase. It would probably be helpful to make a list, she thought, ambling her way towards the house. Maybe that was what she should spend the afternoon doing.

Despite their rocky start, Holly was now in possession of a front door key to Ben's house and, since his comment about it being *their house* that weekend, she had been trying to adopt that mentality a little more. So rather than heading to hers, she opened the front door to Ben's and was surprised to find the upstairs light on, and Ben fussing around.

"Hey, I didn't think you'd seen my messages," he yelled from the top of the stairs. "I was worried I wasn't going to get to see you before I go."

"You're going somewhere?" Holly said, kicking off her shoes then climbing the stairs.

"Did you not read my messages?" Ben's head appeared momentarily in the bedroom doorway before it disappeared again. "I've got a client meeting in London. It's all a bit last minute. I'll be away tonight and tomorrow probably, and I might have to stay on the Friday night. I'll know for certain later on. Anyway, Georgia is picking me up in five minutes, so I need to get ready."

"Georgia? Who's Georgia?"

"The manager at the Stow branch. You must have heard me talk about her. She's on a training program to shift over to personal finance, hence she's been coming to all the events with me for the last four months."

"She has?"

Since falling pregnant, Holly had discovered that baby-brain was a real thing. Or at least she believed it was. She'd certainly been a lot more forgetful over the last couple of months, from small things, like where she'd placed her keys, to bigger things like double ordering peppermint cream boxes for the shop. Although whether this poor memory was because of the excess of hormones running through her body or the fact that she was trying to mentally juggle far too much, she couldn't be sure. As such, there was a very good chance Ben had mentioned someone called Georgia, because the truth was that she tended to switch off when he was talking about the bank.

"I'm so sorry it's so last minute, but I'll definitely be back for the antenatal class on Saturday." He rushed past her to pick up a travel wash bag from the bathroom. "You'll stay here, right? Maybe you could invite Caroline around one evening. You know, really make it feel like it's your place. I mean *our place.*"

"Thanks," Holly said, feeling suddenly confused by all the rushing around her. "I guess that would be nice."

"And I'll give you a call when I get to the hotel."

He stopped for less than a second to put his hands on her belly. "You'll be okay, won't you? I mean, it's still over a month to go, but you can ring me if you think anything's wrong, okay?"

"I'll be fine. We'll be fine." Holly said. Immediately, Ben got back to grabbing pairs of folded socks from his draw and packing them in his bag. A month. One month until their lives changed completely. Though that thought had only just start taking hold in her mind, when another one cut across it. "What about our session on Friday with Dr Ellis? You know that's already booked and paid for."

For the first time since she had come home, Ben fully stopped what he was doing. It was obvious from the look on his face, this was something he hadn't thought of.

"Bugger, I'd completely forgotten about that. Maybe you could go on your own. You might find it really helpful."

"Go to couples' counselling on my own?"

With a hard bite on his bottom lip.

"Maybe. I mean, you have plenty issues you can talk about. And I'm sure Dr Ellis won't mind. Either that, or cancel."

For some reason, his words caused a stiffening in Holly. Was he implying that she was the only one with issues in their relationship? It certainly sounded like that. She was wondering if there was some way she could word this to him without coming across as defensive when a car horn beeped outside.

"That'll be Georgia," Ben said, kissing her again on the forehead and racing down the stairs. "I don't want to keep her waiting."

"Okay, it's fine. You go."

As Ben raced down the stairs, Holly held the bannister and wobbled down slowly behind him. By the time she reached the front door, Ben had already slipped on his shoes and was outside, opening the passenger door to a brand new looking convertible. The car itself was striking, but it was nothing compared to the woman inside. Behind the wheel was possibly the most beautiful woman Holly had ever seen in her life. With dark hair and skin and a smile so radiant, she looked like she should be on the cover of Vogue, rather than living in the Cotswolds and working at a bank.

With his bag in the car, he came back to the house where he wrapped his arms around Holly's waist, before lowering his head and planting a kiss on her bump.

"Remember, if there's anything you need, just call me. I'll have my phone on silent in the meetings, but I'll know if it rings. The guys all know the situation."

Holly nodded. His previous comment and now the distraction of this woman muddying her thoughts.

"I guess I'll see you when you get back," she said. A minute later and she was on her own.

CHAPTER SIXTEEN

Holly was being ridiculous. She had told herself she was being ridiculous time and time again, but still she couldn't stop her mind from wandering. And it wasn't wandering to good places. Every time the shop was empty her thoughts drifted to Ben and the beautiful Georgia and wondering exactly what type of business meetings they were having. And whether it involved being alone together in one of their hotel rooms.

"Stop it!" she said aloud, only afterwards spotting a couple standing in the doorway of the shop waiting to come in. "Sorry, I didn't mean you. I was just talking to myself." Given how she sounded, even to herself, Holly wasn't surprised when the couple backed out of the shop and made a hasty retreat.

With a loud sigh, she dropped on the chair that had been brought down from upstairs and rubbed her ankles. Thursday was always a quiet day and quite often she did it on her own. Her dad sometimes helped for a couple of hours in the afternoon, but given how quiet it had been that morning, she had rung him and told him not to bother. Now she regretted the decision. At least having Arthur in the shop would have stopped her from being entirely alone with her thoughts.

Did Georgia always go away on these trips with Ben, she wondered? And if they were chummy enough to share lifts, why hadn't he ever introduced them?

Her stream of thought was interrupted by a text message, and Holly felt a twinge of something akin to guilt. Giles hadn't messaged her at all that day, and she was now feeling bad about how she was handling the situation. As such, she had promised herself that the next time he messaged she would reply and apologise, it was just better this way. But rather than Giles, it was Caroline that had messaged.

Sorry, can't do Friday night, she said. *Wedding anniversary meal.*

Holly's first thought was how she didn't even know when her best friend's wedding anniversary was. In her defence, they had drifted apart for a long time, and weren't in contact when Caroline and Michael got married. Still, they had been back in contact for well over a year now. She would need to get them a card and some flowers, too. Chocolates were too lazy a gift, especially considering Caroline worked at the shop and got an employee discount.

Upon finding Caroline was busy and unable to spend tomorrow night with her, Holly messaged Jamie, although she could have already predicted the answer that was going to come. Fin had family visiting over from America and Jamie had been spending every spare evening getting to know them. For all the doubts that Holly had had about Fin, she would admit she was a hundred percent wrong. Jamie was now included in a WhatsApp group with his sister and mother and had already been asked to be a bridesmaid at his English cousin's wedding the following spring. It was a far cry from the welcome Ben's sister, Jess, gave Holly.

It had been bad when Ben and Holly were just dating, but when she found out about the baby, it got even worse. It was like Jess was certain Holly had tried to trap him. Which she definitely had not. Paying for the antenatal class had been a controlling act, rather than a supportive one, even if Ben tried to tell Holly otherwise. If only she could swap Ben's sister Jess, for Giles' sister Faye. She had been far more welcoming. She had actually wanted Holly to date Giles. Not that she would ever do that. Not again.

Yet she stared at her phone intently, as if thinking of Giles might cause him to text, even though she had told herself repeatedly that was not what she wanted. When her phone finally buzzed again, it was Jamie telling Holly she already had a whole bunch of plans over the next week and a half, but could be free for just the two of them a week on Tuesday if that worked for her?

Groaning, Holly pushed herself up to her feet, and grabbed a jar of flying saucers. Maybe a bit of sugar would be enough to lighten the mood. Particularly as Ben wasn't there to ration it.

By the time she got home, every inch of her was throbbing. If the swelling in her feet didn't go down soon, she was going to wear her slippers to work. Or maybe bring a beanbag to put by the window to sit in. Then again, that would most likely scare all the customers away, and there wasn't much chance she'd be able to get up out of it again, anyway.

It was going to be a night of takeaway and Netflix, she decided. Relegating a shower to the following morning, she changed straight into her pyjamas when she arrived home. After all, she wasn't going to get many more opportunities to do that when the baby came along. Then again, maybe she wouldn't get out of her pyjamas at all then.

She had just settled down with a new episode of Bake Off and her chicken chow mien when her phone buzzed.

I take it you're ignoring me. Is it something in particular I've done, or just my regular contemptuous self that has upset you?

Holly chuckled to herself.

Just your regular contemptuous self, she went to reply, only to delete the message. Anything hinting of humour would result in a back-and-forth banter that, without Ben here, could go on for hours. The last thing she wanted to do was to slip into a hole like that. But she had promised herself that she was going to be honest. She was going to make a clean cut from this friendship. After all he'd done, he deserved that much.

I think we should stop talking. She read the message over, then hit send before she could chicken out. A moment later, the message was read, and she stared at the phone, waiting for the response. A minute passed. Then two. Nothing came. Not even the string of dots that told her he was composing a reply. Nothing at all. After three minutes, she couldn't take it any longer.

You understand, don't you? She wrote.

Once again, the message was read immediately, although this time a response followed.

I thought we weren't going to talk anymore?

A smile crept on the corner of her lips.

Git she replied.

That's a bit harsh, don't you think? You're the one that imposed these rules. I also feel I should point out that you're the one continuing this conversation. Whereas I was being entirely respectful and abiding by your wishes.

Holly read through the message. Was he winding her up? He was probably winding her up. It was what he did best. Still, she sent him a repeat of her previous message, just in case.

You do understand don't you?

This time a message didn't ping straight back. She could see the little dots there, only every now and then they disappeared. Did that mean he had deleted what he had written, she wondered. She always assumed that when the dots disappeared it was because the person on the other end had deleted whatever it was they had written, but what could Giles have put that he didn't want her to see? They were completely honest with each other, weren't they? She had assumed that they were. She could feel the agitation building within her when the message came through.

I get it.

She waited for some kind of follow up. A quick retort or a winking emoji, but one minute passed and then another and still nothing. Was that it? Was that all he was going to do? Not even a single kiss at the end of their very last message. It must be hormones, she tried to tell herself as a dull ache spread across her chest. Why else would she be feeling like this? She wanted to make things work with Ben. Hadn't she spent the entire morning paranoid that Ben's trip to London involved him having a secret affair with the beautiful Georgia? Why else would she be feeling like that if she didn't love him?

But now things with her and Giles were done. What did that mean? As good as her friends were, these last few months had been the most difficult she had experienced in a long time, and with everyone so close to Ben, the only person she really felt like she could speak honestly with was Giles. Maybe she could use the solo counsellor appointment that week to bring it up. Then again, maybe that wouldn't be a good idea, what with the fact that Dr Ellis saw both her and Ben. What if in their next session together, the good doctor accidentally let Giles' name slip and then where would Holly be?

She was deciding whether she wanted to attend the counselling session on her own, or just cancel as Ben had suggested when her phone beeped again.

Any chance of one last food shop? My fridge is incredibly empty?

A smile flitted across her lips. It was then she realised she had wanted him to put up at least a bit of a fight. To make it seem like he was as sad about the situation as she was. She typed her reply, only to change her mind. The next line she wrote she sent before she could stop herself.

I think maybe it's best if we don't, she wrote. Then, to make sure she didn't go back on herself, she switched her phone to silent and stuck her fork into her chicken chow mien. Strangely, though, her appetite was distinctly diminished.

CHAPTER SEVENTEEN

After picking apathetically at the container of noodles for half an hour, Holly gave up. For some reason, she just wasn't in an eating mood. She wasn't in a watching television mood either. What she really fancied doing was baking, but that required being on her feet and after a full day on her own at the shop, she couldn't bear the thought of standing up any longer. So instead, she switched her phone back on and flicked through social media. Two of her old university friends had had babies in the last month and her news feed was full of photos of chubby legs and babies dressed as dinosaurs. She wasn't going to be like that. Plain baby grows. That would do. Anything else was a waste of money. Unless they were given as gifts, of course. Someone else had posted photos of a new house they had bought. By the looks of things, it had at least five bedrooms. And with a garden that size, they probably needed a ride-on lawnmower. She was about to have a nose at some of the comments when her phone rang.

"Hey?" she said, lifting her voice as she answered the call. "I was expecting you to call before now. Is everything all right?"

Rather than an answer, she received a loud throat clearance. "Ben?"

Wherever he was, it was—judging by the echoing that came from that single cough—a large open space. A hotel foyer, Holly thought. A hotel foyer with Georgia–she quickly quashed the thought. "Is everything alright, where are you?"

"Can you hear me?" Ben's voice rattled down to her.

"I can hear you. Where are you? Is everything okay?"

There was more background noise distorting his words. It had to be a busy hotel, Holly considered. Or perhaps they were in a restaurant or pub.

"I'm really sorry, I don't have much time to talk," Ben said, a resonance to his voice implying he had cupped the phone to make it easier to speak to her. "The train is going in ten minutes and we still need to get to the platform."

"The train? Where are you going? Are you coming home?" Holly said. "Are you coming back tonight?"

This time, the cough was harder and far more deliberate. "Actually, I'm going to Paris," Ben said.

"Sorry?" Holly was certain she had to have misheard him.

"It's all very last minute. We're taking the Eurostar."

"To Paris?"

Paris had been the cause of Holly and Ben's first real argument. The one city that Ben had absolutely refused point blank ever to go to. Holly had taken it as a sign that he wasn't committed to their relationship, though in the end, she learned exactly why he was so opposed to going to the place; it was fair to say it held horrific memories, and he was justified in wanting to avoid that particular city. As such, she had been fine with it. After all, having spent most of her twenties saving for a house and life that had never materialised, there were plenty of places in the world that she and Ben could travel to. Plenty of European cities that held no memories at all.

"Are you going to be okay?" she asked, suddenly feeling a deep sense of apprehension for all he had faced. "I know how much you don't want to go there."

"It's not like I have a choice. It's a work thing," he replied.

"You could say you can't go."

"I can't do that. Besides, this might be good long term. You know, the more I think about it, the more I think it might actually help. Clear out some of the old memories there."

Holly nodded, although her throat tightened by a fraction. Wasn't that the exact thing she had suggested before? A comment that he had dismissed with barely any consideration at all.

"Do you even have your passport with you?" she said, the logistics of the situation springing to mind.

"Yes, luckily. One of the bosses said it was a good idea to bring it along. Things like this have happened before. Something this particular client likes to do."

"Oh, okay. Well, that's good, I suppose," she replied, thinking it was strange Ben didn't at least mention the possibility of this trip if he had taken his passport with him. However, with announcements ringing loudly over the PA system in the background of their conversation, it didn't feel like the right moment to bring it up.

"I've sent a text to Jamie and Caroline, just so they know to be on high alert. And your mum and dad have seen it, too."

Holly bit her tongue. So not only was Ben fine to go to Paris, so fine that he had taken his passport without even mentioning the possibility to her, he also found time to let everyone else know before speaking to her.

"You messaged them before you rang me?" Holly said, firmly.

"I just put out a quick ping on the group chat."

"What group chat?"

"You know, the one I set up should you need any help with the baby or anything."

Her jaw dropped open.

"You set up a WhatsApp group to molly coddle me?"

"No, no."

"Then why are my mum and dad in a group chat that I'm not?"

A short pause followed her question.

"Look, I'm sorry, I should have added you. I just didn't want you to have anything else to worry about. We hardly ever use it."

Jaw still open, Holly sucked in a long, deep breath. What was it the counsellor said to do in moments like this? Moments when Ben tried to take complete and utter control of her and the baby's lives? She closed her eyes, drawing in another lungful of air. *Remind yourself why he's doing this,* Holly said the words over loudly in her head. *Remember that this is his way of coping.*

"Holly, are you there?" His voice brought her back to the moment.

"I'm still here."

"Sorry. I should have thought about the message. I just didn't know how long I was going to have."

"It's fine," Holly said, blowing out her breath and feeling the tension dissipate by a fraction. "I know you were only doing what you think was best. But I am perfectly capable of managing everything."

"I know. I know you are." It was his turn to pause, although the background noise had grown substantially louder. "Look, I really have to go. The others are waiting."

"It's fine. Honestly, I am completely fine. You don't have to worry."

"Okay, I better go. I don't want to miss the train. It might be harder for me to get a signal and things over there, but I'll let you know as soon as I arrive at the hotel. Okay? Love you."

"Lo—"

Holly didn't even get the first word out before the line went dead.

She stared at her phone, and the now blank screen, and knew exactly who she was going to call.

CHAPTER EIGHTEEN

"I still can't believe you set up a chat group to talk about me."

"That wasn't what happened," Caroline insisted as she swept up a spilled bag of sherbet pips from the floor. That was one good thing about being heavily pregnant, Holly decided. She could delegate the jobs she really hated doing, like sweeping the floor, and didn't have to feel bad about it. Although the way she was currently feeling, she would have given Caroline the grottiest tasks even if she hadn't been pregnant. "We talked about this last night on the phone. I didn't even notice you weren't in it until you mentioned it."

Caroline had been the person Holly phoned when she learned about the existence of the secret group chat. Jamie was absent minded with things like that. And she was probably in over fifty different group chats for all her different activities. But Caroline… Holly trusted Caroline to be on top of things like that.

"Who else is in it?" Holly asked, still refusing to let it go.

"I don't know. Us lot. Fin, Michael, your parents."

"Fin and Michael are on it? Really?"

Holly was chewing her way through a bag of hard caramels. There was a good chance she was going to end up with some severe cavities after today, but the more she thought about it, the crosser she had become.

"How long has it been set up?"

While Holly was staring directly at Caroline as she spoke, her friend was now looking intently at the ground, despite the fact that Holly couldn't see a single sherbet pip left to sweep up. "Well?"

"I don't know. A think it was a week or so after you found out about the baby. Maybe after Ben met your parents properly."

"That was months ago."

"It's not like we exchange messages that often. I mean, I posted a couple of things about furniture and stuff I had, but I'd already told you that in the shop. Honestly, this isn't a big deal."

Popping another caramel in her mouth, she chewed the matter over, literally. Was it that big a deal? No, probably not. In some situations, it could probably be considered quite sweet. But she and Ben were constantly talking about communication in their counselling sessions. Every week, that and Ben's need to control everything were the two issues that arose. The thought was like an alarm clock going off in her mind.

"You know, I should get going. I don't know where dad is. This isn't like him. Perhaps the bus is late."

"It's really not a problem," Caroline replied. "I'm sure he'll be here soon. Besides, it's not that busy. Honestly, you go."

Holly looked at her phone and considered ringing her dad one last time, but there really wasn't that much point. His phone was probably on silent—if it was on him at all. It drove her mad; how anyone, even someone her father's age, could get through life without their phone on them was a mystery to her.

"I'll text Mum," Holly said, firing off a quick message to Wendy.

Is Dad okay? He's not here yet.

Unlike Arthur, Wendy was now keeping her phone with her at all times, and had been doing since finding out Holly was pregnant. Obviously, she was determined not to miss the call the moment it came. She could have bet her life that Wendy agreed with Ben's secret chat group, even if no one else did.

Temporary traffic lights on the Fosse. Her mum's message pinged back almost immediately. *I'm sure he'll be there any second.*

Holly read the message out to Caroline.

"See, I told you it would all be fine. Honestly, you go. And don't slate Ben too much while he's not there. He's doing the best he can."

In the car, Holly considered what Caroline had said to her. She didn't moan about Ben, did she? She didn't think she did. After all, she'd hardly whinged about the fact that he had gone to Paris, considering how irritated she had the right to be at that. Instead, she'd been rather calm, all things considered. It was this group that got to her. Keeping things from her. Trying to control her. That was what it felt like.

As she turned off the main high street in Moreton and down the road that led to the fire station, her phone buzzed. She glanced down at the screen, expecting to see her dad's name, or possibly the shop number, but instead, it was Giles' name that flashed up.

She pressed her lips together and declined the call. They may have texted occasionally, and had their weekly shopping date, but they never rang each other. That was just a step too far.

After parking the car up outside the counsellors' office, the phone rang again.

"What are you doing?" she said aloud to the vibrating phone. Had he heard that Ben was in Paris? No, that couldn't be the case. Besides, he knew that Fridays were the day of their couples' counselling before they met for their shopping trip. Perhaps that was it. Perhaps he wanted to tell her he was going to turn up, anyway. She gritted her teeth as she stared at the screen. At best, he was being reckless, ringing her at a time when Ben could see. At worst, he was being damn manipulative, putting thoughts of him into her head right before she and Ben went to work on their relationship. A bitter snort rattled from her lungs. That would most likely be it. She had told him it was over. She had told him that there was no way she could carry on seeing him, and now he was ringing at the one time he knew for certain that she was likely to be with Ben. She would have laughed if it hadn't been so pitiful; of course, a leopard couldn't change its spots, so why the hell had she ever thought Giles would be able to?

Once again declining the call, she moved her thumb to switch it off altogether. Right now, Giles Caverty was making it even easier than ever to cut this relationship off for good.

Ben had been right. The solo counselling session did help. The talk helped Holly address how she wasn't always as open and honest with Ben as she thought she was, and not just about the Giles issue—which she obviously didn't mention. She talked about the secret group chat, and how much it felt like he was trying to manipulate her from behind the scenes. And that he had taken his passport to London, without mentioning to her that it was possible that he could end up going out of the country.

"So, what do you think is causing this behaviour?" Dr Ellis asked after several minutes of nodding her head and jotting down notes.

"I don't need to think about it, I know," Holly said, bluntly. "He's controlling. He's always been controlling."

"Okay, and why do you think he's so controlling?"

She knew the answer to this one too, but still she made a sucking noise before finally managing an answer.

"Because he's scared. He's scared of something happening to me and the baby."

"Right, so what can you do to help with this situation so that he feels secure and you don't feel pressure?"

The remainder of the session was spent going over conversation starters that Holly could have with Ben when he returned. Conversation starters that would be non-confrontational, but still get across the point that she was definitely annoyed. By the time the session finished, she was feeling fairly confident that the issue could be resolved when Ben returned, although all thoughts of Ben disappeared when she switched her phone back on.

Twenty-seven missed calls, she saw on the screen. Twenty-seven. The session was forty minutes long, meaning someone had rung her every minute and a half. It only took a swipe of her finger to see who.

"What the hell," she said. A couple of missed calls from her mum, but ninety percent of them were from Giles. What the hell did he think he was playing at?

She was about to call and ask exactly that when the phone rang again.

"What are you doing?" she said, spitting down the phone. "I could have been with Ben?"

She waited for an answer. An explanation as to why Giles would act in such a manner, but the answer she got wasn't the one she expected at all.

"Holly, you need to get to the hospital. It's your dad, he's had a heart attack. I'm coming to get you now."

CHAPTER NINETEEN

He had arrived less than two minutes after they finished their phone call. Roaring down the road in his four by four, he screeched to a halt parked up next to her, at which point Holly jumped in without even giving it a second thought.

"What happened?" she said, her own heart hammering in her chest as she clipped in her belt. "Where is he? Is he okay?"

"They've taken him to Cirencester," Giles told her, doing a U-turn in the road as he spoke. "Your mum went straight there. I told her I'd come and get you."

"I don't understand." Holly couldn't wrap her head around it. It was difficult enough trying to make sense of the fact that Arthur had had a heart attack, the fact that Giles was here too was all too much to process. "Where did you see them? Were you at the hospital too?" It was the only explanation that could make any sense to her; that Giles was at the hospital visiting his sister, but she worked at Cheltenham, didn't she? Not Cirencester. And she was a midwife.

"I was at your parents' house when your mum got the telephone call," Giles said, staring with intense concentration at the road ahead. Unfortunately, his answer only deepened Holly's confusion.

"What do you mean? Why were you at my parents'? What were you doing there?"

This time he didn't answer straight away, but reached into his pocket and pulled out a small brown envelope.

"I was returning this," he said, giving Holly a second to open it. Inside, she found a single earring. It was her earring, one that Ben had given her, but why Giles had it, it took her a moment to recall.

"From shopping," she said, remembering that moment in the shop a week ago, when his hand had brushed her hair to retrieve the item. "When the back fell off, and I didn't have anywhere to put it."

"I got you a replacement back for it," Giles said. "I was going to return it when we next went shopping, but… well you know…" Holly picked the earring up and turned it over in her hand. The gold stud was fitted with a bright green stone and there, on the back, a brand new shiny butterfly. For a reason, she couldn't explain a lump stuck in the back of her throat.

"I thought it was easier if I dropped it at your parents," Giles said quietly, breaking the silence. "I thought someone might see me if I came to your house. I didn't think you'd appreciate being put in that position."

"Thank you," she whispered. The lump was going nowhere, forcing itself higher up and causing tears to prick her eyes.

"It's the least I could do. But when I reached the front door, your mum was just coming out."

For a split second, Holly had been so absorbed in the earring and the thought of Giles at her parents' house that she had forgotten about her dad. But the thoughts returned with a thud.

"What happened? Where was he?"

"On the bus, apparently. One of the other people noticed, and the driver did a detour and took him straight to the hospital. Your mum was a state, obviously, so I offered to drive her to the hospital, but one of the neighbours had already made the same offer."

"So you came and got me," Holly whispered.

"Wendy was trying to call you, but I thought it was easier if she had one less thing to worry about."

The lump had fully blocked her throat now, and tears were pricking Holly's eyes, one escaping, then another down her cheek. Giles' hand left the gear stick and reached across to take hers.

"Thank you," Holly whispered.

Silence settled between them, though Holly couldn't sit still. Her feet were tapping in the footwell, while her eyes darted constantly to the dashboard to see how fast they were going. There wasn't any traffic and Giles was edging towards the wrong side of the speed limit, but it didn't feel like they were getting anywhere. Why the hell was it taking so long?

"I know you want to call quits on whatever this is," he said, taking his eyes off the road for a second so that he could look straight at her. "But I want you to know that I'm here for you. Whenever you need me, I'll always be here for you."

A thousand unspoken words passed through the air between them as Holly waited for the light-hearted quip to break the tension. One of his characteristic slanted smiles or crude insults, that told her he was just winding her up. That assured her she was one of a hundred girls that he used his flattery on, but the moment stretched out between them, with his hand on hers, their fingers dangerously close to interlocking. She shifted in her seat and slid her hand out from underneath his, suddenly focusing her attention on the passing scenery outside, trying to control all the thoughts and images of her dad that flashed through her head.

"Okay, this is you," Giles said, breaking Holly's concentration a few minutes later.

Her head snapped upwards. After the seemingly slow journey, the hospital had suddenly crept up on her. They were weaving their way around the circus of roundabouts into the hospital grounds.

"There's a long stay car park just over the side of the road. I'll park up there. Then give me a ring when you're done and I can drive you back to Moreton to pick up your car."

"You don't have to do that. I can get the bus."

"I want to do that. You've got to get back to Moreton for your car, remember? The bus would take ages. You don't want to be doing that in your condition. I don't want you doing that."

She bit down on her lip. Perhaps it was being at the hospital and about to see her dad, or the hormones that were doing a number on her, but there was no stopping the tears now they'd started.

"I don't want you to do that," she said quietly. "I don't want to know that you'll be there for me. I don't want to know that you're always there."

He nodded, then lifted her hand and used his thumb to brush away her tears as one trickled down her cheek. "How about just this one last time, then?" he said. "Just this one last time, then you can be rid of me. Sound like a deal?"

She stepped out of the car and turned back to the door.

"Go home, Giles."

CHAPTER TWENTY

The strip lighting in the hospital glared overhead. Why did they use that type of lighting? Would it hurt to make the place feel a little less clinical and cold? Maybe something to mask the scent of caustic cleaning fluids burning her throat.

"Is everything all right?" A nurse appeared at Holly's side, looking at her bump with concern. "Do you need to sit down? How far apart are the contractions?"

"Contractions?" Holly took a second to realise what she was saying.

"Oh no, I'm fine. I'm not here for me. My father was brought in. He had a heart attack, I think." Just saying the words out loud was enough for her own heart to start racing again. "He was on a bus. He was on a bus when he had the heart attack. His name's Arthur Berry."

"Okay." The nurse placed her hand on Holly's shoulder. "You just take a seat and I'll go find where he's been taken. Is that alright? You can take a seat just over there."

She pointed to the row of chairs currently half filled with

adults and children. Some were hacking audibly, while others clutched various parts of their bodies and whimpered softly. She moved to sit, only to decide that standing was what she wanted to do. She had been sitting in her counselling session, then again in Giles' car. What she needed to do was walk.

In less than five minutes, the nurse returned and told Holly which ward her father had been moved to. Although she glanced down more than once at her bump while giving her instructions to get there, offering the impression she thought she was going to be admitted shortly herself.

Upon arriving at the correct ward she found an elderly nurse seated behind the high white desk struggling to stifle a yawn.

"I'm here to see Arthur Berry," she said breathlessly. "I was told he was here. He had a heart attack. I'm his daughter."

"Sorry, could you say the name again, please?"

Holly opened her mouth, ready to repeat her father's name, but before she could get a word out, a voice called out from further down the corridor.

"Holly!"

Never in Holly's life had Wendy looked so frail. Her skin was ashen, and dark circles ringed her eyes.

"Mum."

The moment they embraced Wendy dissolved into tears, her sobbing frame rocking against Holly for nearly a minute before she straightened up again.

"Thank goodness you're here."

"Has he really had a heart attack?"

"A mild one, thankfully. He's okay. The doctors say it's a wake-up call more than anything. But he's going to need to take it easy. I don't know when he'll be able to come back to work for you."

"Mum, that is not a priority at all. Can I see him? Is he awake?"

Her answer came in the form of her father's voice.

"Yes, I am awake and I can hear you two chatting," Arthur called from inside the room. "Having a heart attack didn't make me deaf." The two women shared weak, watery smiles, their hands now squeezing one another tightly.

"I guess you should come in and see him," Wendy replied.

There were six beds in the room, and currently, all the curtains were open around them. In four of the beds the patients were sleeping, but in the one closest to the window, a young woman was sitting up and laughing, surrounded by a group of friends or family.

Holly wasn't sure what she expected when she saw her dad. This year she had had visited hospitals more than the last ten years of her life combined; what with Verity's trip and fall, then her own tumble that landed her in Cheltenham general and now this.

"Now, don't look like that," Arthur said, as Holly's eyes immediately welled with tears. "I'm fine. I'm absolutely fine."

"You could have died, Dad." Her voice croaked as she choked on the words.

"Honestly, I'm good. Bit of a shock to the system. That's all. Don't you worry about me. Your mother's the one you should be worried about. All this bloody crying she's been doing. Can't be doing her no good at all." Given the similar shades of grey they had turned, he could be right; it was hard to tell whether Arthur or Wendy had had the heart attack. "You mark my words, I'll be back on that shop floor, up and down those stairs again, by Monday."

"You will not," Wendy said sternly. "Two weeks, complete rest. That's what the doctor said. A minimum of two weeks.

And don't think you're going back to all those lunch time trips to the bakery whenever you fancy it either. Or helping yourself to whatever you want from the shelves. It'll be salad, fish and vegetables every day from now on. I'm making an appointment with the dietician myself."

With a sweeping roll of his eyes, Arthur offered Holly a sidelong smile, but she couldn't respond. She had gone past thinking about him working in the shop, or if that even mattered. There were bigger, more important things to think of.

"You're going to be a grandad in a few weeks, Dad," she whispered. "You're going to be a grandad."

Arthur's smile dropped as he took Holly's hand. A serious look clouding his face for the first time since she had entered the room.

"I know, love. I do. And I promise you. I'm not going anywhere. I'm going to be the best damn grand-pappy that little thing could ever ask for. I mean that. Even if it does mean eating salads every day."

"And no chocolate or sweets? You'll do that?"

"I'll do anything for you, I promise."

"Good, because I need you. You're the number one man in my life, Daddy. I need you." And just like that, she was sobbing again, though it felt like it was for more than just her father this time.

CHAPTER TWENTY-ONE

After just over an hour, Holly was asked to leave, although she was planning on heading home, anyway. The woman in the corner who had previously been inundated with visitors, was on her own now, and obviously trying to sleep, and though Arthur kept trying to hide the fact that he needed rest too, his eyes kept closing and his head lolled forward. Much the same way as it did when he was supposedly watching Match of the Day on television late at night.

"I'm going to stay here," Wendy said. "Geraldine next door has already said they're going to drop some clean clothes off at reception, so I don't need to worry about that. But I don't want to miss the doctor when he comes on his early morning rounds. You know what your dad is like. He'll miss out all the important information and tell me everything's fine."

Knowing there was no point arguing or suggesting her mum pop home for at least a couple of hours to get some sleep, Holly kissed her on the top of her head before heading outside.

It was a fair walk from Cirencester hospital to the bus stop in the centre of town, and more than once Holly glanced at her phone. She considered calling Jamie or Caroline to see if they could pick her up, then remembered how they each had things on that night. It was fine, she told herself as she took the walk one steady step at a time. She could do with the time on her own. Besides, she should probably ring Ben and tell him what had happened.

The ring tone was unfamiliar, shorter perhaps, and it took Holly a second to remember he was in a different country. Several rings later and Holly was about to give up but then Ben's voice came through from the other end.

"Hey, is everything okay? I'm just in a meeting. Is the baby all right?"

The sentences and questions came out in one breath and Holly wasn't sure which one she was meant to answer first, although it was obvious from his rushing manner that Ben didn't have a lot of time.

"The baby and I are fine. We're both fine, b—" She had barely got the sentence out, when Ben cut across her.

"That's great. That's really great. Can we chat later then?"

Holly blinked repeatedly. Yes, they were both fine, but she did have something important to say. Important to her at least, even if it didn't affect Ben directly, her father was the grandfather to their child. That should matter. Yet for a second time, as she opened her mouth and prepared to tell him about Arthur, Ben's voice beat her to it, although he wasn't speaking directly to her. Instead, he was calling out to someone there with him.

"Sorry, yes, I'll just be a minute. No, don't worry, I'll sort it now. I'm really sorry," he said, his attention and voice now directed back down the phone to Holly. "This is just really bad timing. I'll ring you back, okay? When this meeting is done. I'll ring you back in a couple of hours."

"Oh, okay." Holly said.

"Great, love you."

The line was dead before she could reply.

For the next few minutes she walked numbly along the edge of the main road towards the town centre and the main bus stop, replaying Ben's dismissiveness over and over in her mind. The weight of his words—or lack thereof—added to the already immense mental load she was carrying. Of course, he hadn't meant to upset her. It had just been a normal phone call to him. Why should he have known something had happened to her father? He couldn't have. And yet the distance of his voice caused a hollowness to spread out within her. She could have lost her dad today. What if it had been more than a minor heart attack? What if no one on the bus had noticed him, or the driver hadn't had the sense to divert the bus and take them to the hospital? Would Ben have still hung up the phone so quickly then? Would he have still assumed that as long as the baby was alright that nothing else in the world could possibly have gone wrong? The numbness crept further down her as her chest tightened. A few cold drops of rain hit her arm, though she didn't even register them. She didn't register anything except this insurmountable numbness that was creeping through her. Even when the drizzle picked up the pace and started to form puddles on the ground, she continued to walk on, unaware of it all. She had nearly lost her dad today; she thought again and again. She had nearly lost him. And even though she was in a relationship with a man she knew loved her, and even though she had a baby the size of a watermelon growing in her belly. Even though all of those things, she couldn't remember feeling quite so alone.

As she reached the bus stop, her mind was still so dazed and distracted that she didn't even notice that it was her bus pulling away. She didn't even think to lift a hand to try to stop it, or even quicken her pace by a fraction so that the driver might look in his rear-view mirror and see a pregnant lady trying to chase him down. Instead, she just stopped. The rain sprang up from the puddles on the ground, spraying her ankles. It had already started to run down the back of her neck and drench her top underneath. She needed to move. She needed to sit somewhere and get dry. Yet she just couldn't.

In her dazed state, she didn't even hear the car beeping its horn across the road from her, or notice as the man ran out with a large umbrella in his hand. Only when that umbrella was lifted over her head did she feel the sudden absence of the rain and notice something had changed.

When she looked up, her eyes were so tear filled that the image in front of her was almost entirely blurry, but she didn't need to be able to pick out any details to see the salmon pink colour of his shirt.

"I told you I was fine," Holly said. The sound of her voice making her suddenly more aware of her surroundings and how close she was to crying.

"And I decided I didn't believe you," Giles said, then he wrapped an arm around her shoulder and guided her towards her car.

CHAPTER TWENTY-TWO

Previously, Holly had always assumed that heated seats were an unnecessary luxury in cars, placed there with the single aim of hiking up the price on an already expensive model. But as she sat in the passenger seat of Giles' four by four, the warmth drying her out from every direction, she decided that this was one little luxury she might one day like to indulge in herself.

"You know I hate telling you what to do, but I'm not sure whether you should really have the heated seat on, you know. With the baby and everything. Aren't you meant to avoid conditions that are too warm?"

Holly wriggled in against the comfort of the seat, wishing she could forget what Giles had just said, while trying to recall all the things they had told her in the antenatal class. There was definitely something about overheating. Was it warm baths? Somewhere in the depths of her mind, she recalled Ben telling her about having to be careful in the bath, but was that the position you were sitting in, the heat of the water, or just the fact that it was far easier to go head over heels when you centre of gravity was a foot in front of you? The fact that she couldn't remember only made her more irritated by the whole thing, and with a huff of annoyance, she switched off the heated seat. Thankfully, the residual heat remained.

"You stuck around," she said again. "I told you I'd be fine."

"I know you did, but I had some jobs to do in Cirencester, anyway."

"Really," Holly said, eyeing him suspiciously. "And then you just happened to be parked by the bus stop, conveniently placed to swoop in and rescue me."

"Pure coincidence, I'd just stopped for a sandwich, and then there you were." His voice lacked any real conviction.

"So where is your sandwich?"

She looked into his grey eyes as he shrugged, the numbness that she had been feeling only moments ago, now replaced with a deep appreciation. An appreciation that remained until his face contorted into an expression that Holly had no trouble reading at all. A guilty expression.

"You should probably know…" he started.

"What is it? What have you done?" she said, overlapping him as he started to speak. "What have you done this time?"

His lips pressed together into a thin flat line as his eyes momentarily shifted away from hers.

"I rang the shop."

"You what?"

"Don't get mad at me. I'm sorry. I know you like to be in charge of everything. But when I dropped you off at the hospital, I realised you hadn't called the shop to let them know you wouldn't be back and I didn't want them worrying about you or pestering you. And I guessed that as you hadn't remembered in the car journey over there, you were unlikely to remember once you were with your dad."

He was a hundred percent right. The only time Holly had thought, even fleetingly, about the shop, was when Arthur had mentioned going back to work, and even then it hadn't registered with her that she had left Caroline on her own without any indication of where she had gone or why. After a few seconds grappling with the fact that she hadn't even thought about the shop, another thought struck. Caroline would almost certainly know Giles' voice, which meant questions were bound to come. As in, why was Giles the one who took her, and how did he know where she was? And of course, she could answer them, but then how would she explain the earring of hers he had?

"It's okay. Just in case you're worried, I said I was a neighbour of your parents. I thought it was easier that way." Giles said, as if reading her mind.

Holly blew out a lungful of air in relief. The weight of worry that had been forming on her chest dissipated, although it was quickly replaced with something even harder and deeper. Guilt.

"Thank you," she said, forcing the words up past the lump in her throat. "Thank you for it all."

"It's what I'm here for. After all, isn't that what friends are for?"

Friends. That had never really been a word that fitted well with them. Could you really be friends when you had to sneak about in secret?

They were driving slowly, about to take the roundabout turning that led them to the Fosseway and straight down to Bourton, when Giles turned off and headed instead to the service station.

"If you need petrol, please let me pay," Holly said. "It's the least I can do."

But rather than heading for fuel, Giles turned left into the car park of the service station hotel and switched off the engine.

"Giles?"

"It's just a thought, but before I drive you home, are you sure that's where you want to go? Just, I saw Ben wasn't with you at today's session. Is he at home? I'm not trying to stick my nose in where it isn't wanted, only I don't think you should be at home on your own. Maybe call Jamie first? I'd offer to stay, but I'm guessing that's not up for discussion."

His eyes glinted with a mischief that made her heart flutter, although she tried to stamp the sensation out.

"I don't think that would be the most sensible idea," Holly agreed.

"But will someone be there? You know, if you need anything. Today was quite a shock, and in your condition I don't think that shocks are a good thing. I'd feel a lot happier if I were leaving you, knowing that there were people there to look after you."

As he awaited Holly's answer, she couldn't help but wonder why this felt so different from when Ben was concerned about her. Perhaps it was the way he posed things as a question, rather than a command or an order. Or setting group chats she wasn't a part of.

"You know, I'm never technically on my own anymore," she said, evading the question with a quick rub to her belly. Giles laughed, but it was a short-lived chuckle that quickly faded.

"You know that's not what I mean."

"I know," she said. "But honestly, I don't know if I can even face people tonight. Just the idea of talking to anyone. Even Caroline. I don't think I'd be the best company."

"I get it. But what about food? You haven't got any of your food shopping. I guess you probably don't feel like it right now, but you could give me a list. I can go get whatever it is you need?"

Holly's mind went to her fridge. What was there in it? Probably not much, and certainly nothing she would feel like eating at the moment. But she couldn't send Giles to run errands for her. Not after everything he'd already done for her. Then again, he was probably right about her not being on her own just yet. And like that the solution appeared before her.

"You know what, I could do with getting some food in," she said. "What do you say to one last shop?"

CHAPTER TWENTY-THREE

When Holly had suggested she and Giles go food shopping, it sounded like the perfect option. Giles was right. She didn't want to be on her own in the house after the day she had had, but with all her friends occupied and Ben away, what else could she do? Besides, she needed food. She certainly wasn't in the mood for cooking and if she was left on her own at home… well, there was only so much crying one person could do in a day, and she didn't want to know what that limit was.

While the supermarket was in the Stow-on-the-Wold, they drove straight past it and kept going, having decided it would be best if Holly picked up her car first. That way, she could head straight home after the food shop. The way they normally did.

When they reached Morton, Giles parked up just behind her car, which by some miracle hadn't got a ticket.

"I guess this is where I leave you, for a minute," Giles said, cutting the engine, and leaving his side of the car, ready to open her door. Normally she would hate that—a man opening the car door for her, like she was incapable of doing it herself—but at the moment, she found her legs less than willing to leave the comfort of Giles' car.

Her door swung open, yet she hesitated, bracing her hands on the warm seat.

"I'm fine," she said, noting Giles' immediate look of concern. "I just need a minute, that's all."

With a deep breath in, she spun around on the seat so that her legs were dangling off the side, but the second that she moved to drop, she was hit with a bout of head rush. Her body fell forward, toppling faster than she could control. Fear flashed before her. She was going to hit the ground. The baby was going to hit the ground and there was no way she was going to be able to stop it.

"I've got you. I've got you."

In one sweeping moment, Giles' arms caught her. And rather than hitting the ground face first, as she had thought she was about to, she was there, pressed against his chest, his arms wrapped so tightly around her she couldn't have fallen an inch more even if she wanted to. "I've got you," he whispered again.

Holly was breathless. Her heart racing from the fear of the drop. Inhaling through her nose, she tried to get a good lungful of air, but instead, all she got was a lungful of his aftershave. A deep musky scent that made her head spin in a whole different manner. Hurriedly, she pushed herself back and away from him. With a heat flushing her cheeks, she reached into her handbag to retrieve her car keys. After several seconds of fumbling, she found them at the bottom.

"Sorry about that. I guess my balance isn't what I thought it was." She tried to laugh, but her voice came out tight and breathless and Giles' eyes narrowed on her.

"If you think I am letting you drive anywhere like that, you're insane," he said bluntly, plucking the keys out of her hand before she even realised what was going to happen. There was no denying that her reactions weren't quite what they should be. She hadn't even seen what he was about to do.

"When did you last eat?" he said, his glower still firmly fixed in place.

"Eat?"

"Yes, it's a thing that humans and animals need to do. Consuming food. It stops us from passing out for instance. Particularly important when you're growing something that's sucking all the energy out of you."

There was no humour in his voice, nor his gaze. His eyebrows were raised as he stared at her expectantly, awaiting her answer and Holly found herself feeling like she was back at school being reminded for not doing her homework. Not that she ever did that.

"I don't know. Lunch I suppose."

"You suppose?"

Holly thought about it a little deeper. It had been a rather indulgent morning with sweets, she recalled she had polished off a bag of chocolate covered Brazil before nine this morning. Then there had been the new delivery of flavoured sherbets and she had wanted to try those. As such, she had decided there was no point having an early lunch the way she normally did before her appointments, and had decided she would pick something up in Moreton after the session. Which she hadn't done. Still staring intently at her, Giles didn't bother to wait for an answer. He stepped back, holding the car door wide open.

"Get back in," he said.

"What? No, I'm fine."

"No, you're not fine. And you're obviously not in a place where you can make rational decisions about how you're feeling, so I'm taking you to get something to eat. And please take care getting back in the car, I don't think my back will cope with having to lift you and that massive bump of yours up from the ground." Holly opened her mouth to object, yet she didn't even get the first syllable out. "In. Now."

This time, her stomach growled, and she didn't bother arguing. She turned around, ready to clamber back up into the seat, when Giles pressed his hands squarely above her hips. The effect was instant. The rush of heat. Her throat drying. She stopped abruptly, her heart skipping at such a pass it was a miracle she didn't get dizzy all over again. The grip was so firm. So secure, like he had held her there a thousand times. Holly's breaths stuttered in her chest as she fought the sensation that was running up from his hands. The safety she felt emanating from his grip.

"You're alright, I've got you."

A new tremble afflicted Holly's knees. It was still the lack of food; she tried to convince herself. That was the reason she couldn't think rationally with Giles' hands on her. And Giles' hands were still on her. Holding her upright, supporting her.

"It's fine, I've got this," she said suddenly, hoisting herself with the kind of speed she probably wouldn't have managed before she was pregnant, and freeing herself from Giles' touch.

A second later, he closed the door and headed around the car to the driver's side. Holly closed her eyes and took a deep breath in. It was the stress of the day, she told herself repeatedly as her heart continued to race. She would feel better when she had eaten something. She would definitely think more rationally then, wouldn't she?

CHAPTER TWENTY-FOUR

It was the first time Holly had properly looked at her watch in hours, and she was amazed to find it wasn't as late as she had thought. At six thirty on a Friday, the carpark to the Pickle and Fig was only just starting to fill up with people ready to celebrate the start of the weekend.

"It's up to you if you want to eat outside," Giles said, offering her a hand to help her down out of the car. "They have some good outdoor heaters here, if that's what you'd prefer? It's pretty small inside, but I'm sure they'll be able to find us a table. Holly?"

Holly was only half listening. She was looking around her with a sudden panic growing in her chest. She was about to have dinner with another man when the father of her child was away in a different country. Could she really do that? In her head, she rationalised the situation. She wasn't on a date with Giles. He was taking her to get some food as a friend. He was being a good friend, that was all. A friend when all her others were unavailable. A friend that Ben happened to have a vehement dislike for, that was all.

"They have a back room. Only a couple of tables. Exclusively for locals," Giles said, reading her expression. "If you're really that worried about us being seen together."

"No, no… it's fine. It's fine." Holly wished she could stop the red flush from colouring her cheeks as she forced herself to smile. "It's still fairly quiet. And it's not like I know that many people in Stow. It'll be fine."

A small muscle twitched along Giles' jawline and for a second Holly thought he was going to say something, but he just nodded quickly.

"This way then," he said, taking large strides towards the pub, and for once, not waiting for her.

The inside was far more modern than Holly expected, with large print wallpaper, and vibrant lampshades that hung above dark wooden tables, though it smelt exactly as any pub should. Ales and hops flooded the air around the bar, while the aroma of home cooked food wafted out from the kitchen. She didn't need to see the menu of the food to know that her dad would love it here. An ache immediately spread across her chest. Maybe when he was fully recovered, she could take him here to celebrate. Just for a salad, of course.

"Do your parents need anything dropping off?" Giles said, having stopped in front of her and apparently aware exactly Holly's mind had gone from her glazed look. "I don't mind picking them up from hospital when he gets out either, if that would be helpful."

"Thank you," Holly said, genuinely meaning it. "They've already asked one of the neighbours, so they've got that sorted."

"Okay, well, just let me know if I can help."

She was tempted to say thank you again, but there were only so many times you could thank someone in such a short time, she decided. Besides, Giles had already headed over to the bar and was busy shaking the barman's hand.

"Good to see you, Frank," Giles said.

"Been a while," Frank replied with a throaty cackle. "Take it you've been up to the usual mischief?"

"Me? Mischief?" Giles offered him his best grin. A grin that had to have melted at least a thousand hearts. Although Holly was obviously immune to it now. "Any chance of a table for two?" Giles carried on. "Out back, if you've got it."

"Always got room for you, fella," Frank said, about to turn when his eyes reached Holly and bulged at the sight of the bump.

"Is there something I should know?" he said, unable to stop his jaw from dropping.

"Nothing to do with me," Giles replied. "Trust me, that is significantly more than I can handle. I'm just babysitting. Literally."

The barman raised his eyes from Holly's bump to look at her directly, at which point he offered a small smile. "Well, any friend of Giles' is always welcome here. There's a free table out the back. Menu is on the chalkboard," he pointed.

Holly turned around to see the chalkboard in question. Three feet high, it was covered in local pub staples, like gammon, egg and chips, trout with new potatoes, specialty burger and the like.

"What do you recommend?" Giles said. "Jenny cooked up anything special?"

"Doesn't she always? If I were you, I'd go for the venison. Nice bit of fillet. Proper nice, but we didn't manage to get that much in."

"In that case, I shall have the venison. Holly, what do you want?"

There was so much to choose from Holly was struggling to decide. It didn't help that she felt both starving hungry from lack of food and nauseous from the stress of the day.

"I'd just like a plate of chips," she said, and which Giles scoffed.

"Do I need to remind you why we're here? You need a proper meal. Can we get a plate of chips and one of your burgers too, please?" He looked at Holly. "You eat burgers, right?"

"I… yes."

"And make it a big portion," Giles continued to Frank. "Extra of all the sides."

"I'm really not hungry," Holly insisted.

"Then don't eat it," Giles replied bluntly. "But you've never had one of Jenny's burgers. Trust me, you'll want it all."

He was right. Even if Holly hadn't been absolutely famished, she would have polished off every last morsel of the burger.

"I'm not one for grand statements," she said, placing her knife and fork down on the completely cleared plate. "But that was the best burger I've ever eaten in my life."

"I told you."

They had taken one of the three tables in the area to the rear of the bar, and there's was the only one occupied. Holly had taken the seat that faced inwards, offering a view back across the bar and to the main restaurant area. Even though she knew the likelihood of anyone coming in and seeing her was almost zero, it was a relief to know that with this seating arrangement she would be able to spot them far quicker than they would be able to spot her.

"I don't think I'm ever going to eat another burger again." She said, her mind still lost on the deliciousness of the meal.

"I'll just be disappointed." She leant back on the chair and rested her hand on her belly, that for the first time in a long time, didn't feel like it was only a bump.

"Well, maybe I can bring you here again sometime?"

"That would be nice."

They both realised what they had said at the exact same time, and Holly went from feeling satisfyingly stuffed to altogether awkward. Giles, too, seem lost for words as he stared down at his plate. When his head came back and his eyes met hers, they shone with a seriousness Holly had rarely, if ever, seen from him.

"I don't think I ever properly apologised for everything that happened," he said.

"You did. When you interrupted my pizza, remember?"

A smile toyed on the corner of his lips, but didn't fix.

"I should have apologised more. I should have grovelled."

"I would like to see that," Holly laughed. "Giles Caverty grovelling. I'm pretty sure I could sell tickets for that event." She chuckled, expecting his response to be the same, but his expression remained as forlorn and deadpan as it had before.

"I mean it," he said. "What I did to you, it was so low. It was beyond low. I look back at the person I was then and…" He shuddered, a visual representation of the words he couldn't express otherwise. "I think that's why seeing you has been so important to me. It keeps me in check, you know? Reminds me of that person. Reminds me of who I never want to be again. It reminds me of what I lost."

The silence bloomed again, and Holly could sense there was so much more he wanted to say. Things that couldn't be said. There were things she wanted to say, too. How she looked forward to their accidental shopping meetings every week because it gave her a chance not to be perfect. To swear and whine about how much her ankles hurt and not feel ungrateful. She looked forward to the shopping trips because she knew that however bad the session with Ben and Dr Ellis had gone before, and however many serious conversations were waiting for her when she got home, that Giles would make her laugh and forget about it, even if it was only for a short while. She wanted to say that it was one of the parts of the week that she looked forward to the most and that she wished they could do things like that more often. Frequently even. But just as she was about to tell him she noticed a flash of blond hair on the other side of the bar and then heard a familiar cackling laugh shoot across the bar, and what she actually said instead was, "Shit."

CHAPTER TWENTY-FIVE

Holly couldn't move or speak. The heaven that had been the burger was instantly forgotten, and for a solid minute the only words that rolled through her head were expletives. What the hell was Clarissa doing there? Holly stretched a little in her seat, hoping that she was wrong, but no, there she was standing at the bar, hair perfect, with glasses perched on her head, laughing enthusiastically at something Frank the barman was saying.

"Are you okay?" Giles asked, sitting up and stretching his hand across the table to rest upon hers. The spark shot through her skin. Holly hurriedly snatched her hand away and ducked down, ensuring she was suitably hidden.

"Clarissa," Holly hissed. "She's on the other side of the bar. I don't think she saw me, though. Is she still looking in this direction?"

Giles made to turn around, twisting so he could see over his shoulder and across the other side of the bar, but Holly grabbed him by the arm of his shirt and tugged him back down.

"You can't just look!"

"But you just asked me to?"

"She could have seen us."

Her heart was pounding in her chest with the temperature of the room having taken a definite upward turn. How the hell were they going to get out of there without Clarissa seeing her with Giles? Because if Clarissa saw her with Giles it could get back to Ben and she would have to explain about why Giles was at her mum's and the earring and the shopping trips and Holly's head was already spinning considering how much of a disaster that would be. Not to mention, the last time she had seen Clarissa she had thought she was going into labour. She had already text Holly half a dozen times, wanting an update. Eventually Holly had responded with only two words. False alarm.

"Who is she?" Giles asked, once again, trying to peer over his shoulder to get a view across the bar, though this time Holly didn't bother pulling him back down.

"Someone from my antenatal class," Holly whispered back. "This is not good. We need to go." She remained hunched down in her seat, her body close to toppling as she squeezed out from her chair, and grabbed her coat from the back of it. She was trying to make herself as invisible as possible as she moved. Yet despite the urgency of her words and actions, Giles remained seated.

"You want to leave?"

"We need to go. I just said that."

"Now? Do you not want to sit for a bit? You've just eaten."

Giles was speaking, but Holly wasn't listening. Her eyes were fixed on Clarissa, who had just received her first drink from Frank. Any second now she'd move, Holly prayed. She'd turn back to the main seating area and that would be their chance.

"You go out first," she hissed to Giles. "Get the car running. I'll pay. That way, she definitely won't see you."

Giles opened his mouth only to close it again, at which point a deep frown creased his forehead.

"You're serious, aren't you?"

"Please, before she sees us here together. She's got her back turned now. Go. Go!"

Still dawdling in a manner that made Holly's pulse soar, Giles finally stood up.

"At least let me give you my card to pay with?" he said, offering out his wallet. Holly slapped his hand away.

"I can pay. Just go. Go!"

With an expression that was half bemusement and half concern, Giles lifted his jacket off the back of his chair and sauntered out to the front of the bar. How was it possible she was still standing when her pulse was going this fast, Holly wondered momentarily? Any second now, she was going to pass out. Then how would she explain the situation? Would Giles come to the rescue again? She could pretend he was a stranger. Or her brother, perhaps. Yes, Clarissa didn't know she was an only child. She could do that. Holly pressed her hands on Giles' back, pushing him out towards the exit. They were almost there. Any second now, she'd be on her own and Giles safely out of sight.

Giles just disappeared through the doorway as Clarissa turned her head in his direction, then she immediately turned back towards Holly.

"It is you?" Clarissa cried across the bar.

Her stomach plummeted, and a wave of nausea struck. Resigned to defeat she walked over to her.

"Mwah, Mwah, darling," Clarissa said as Holly forced a smile—that probably looked more like a grimace—onto her face .

"Clarissa," she said, in her warmest voice.

"I thought that was you, hiding away back there. How are you after last week. I was telling Floyd all about it. You poor thing. Those Kegels are so important, aren't they? I do mine religiously. On the hour, every hour." Holly's back teeth ground together, though she managed not to say anything. As it happened, Clarissa had plenty more to say. "Anyway, that's enough shop talk. I didn't know you came here. The food's incredible, isn't it? Floyd and I love it. Was that Ben I saw slipping out there?"

With Holly's throat squeezed shut, the first sound that came out was closer to a squeak than an actual word. All the previous thoughts she had had about a brother, or a friend, evaporated.

"Yes. Yes. Ben." Apparently, one syllable at a time was all she could manage.

"I barely recognised him. He looks every so dashing in pink, doesn't he?"

This time Holly couldn't reply at all. A mute nod was all she managed. However, Clarissa had more than enough words to fill any silence. "You should get him to come back in. We can have a drink together. Unless you're in a rush, that is?" It took Holly a second to realise that Clarissa had just given her a way out of the horrendous situation. With something between a gasp and a cough, she finally managed a full sentence.

"I'm sorry. I've actually got to go. We're in a terrible rush. But perhaps another time? Family things, you know." She smiled sweetly, waving her card at Frank as an indication that she wanted to pay. With a nod, Clarissa lifted her drinks from the bar.

"Well, give Ben my love, won't you? And I'll see you tomorrow."

"I cannot wait," she lied. Only when the bill was paid and

she was clambering into the passenger side of Giles' car, did she allow herself a breath of relief.

"Well, that was close," she sighed, turning to Giles, smiling. Yet rather than a smile, he was wearing the biggest scowl she had ever seen.

CHAPTER TWENTY-SIX

For a second, Holly thought she had imagined the hostility, but when Giles turned on the engine and drove out of the carpark and still hadn't said anything to her, Holly took a deep breath in.

"Thank God Frank got us a table out the back."

"Thank God indeed," Giles replied, in a manner than implied he was anything but pleased. She waited for him to say something else, but instead he stared intently at the road.

"Have I done something?" she asked, her voice coming out tentatively quiet.

Giles' eyes remained on the road as he spoke. "Like what?"

"Something to upset you."

His lips twisted, and she knew immediately that she had, although for the life of her, she couldn't think what she had done.

"Is this about leaving without dessert?" she tried tentatively.

"Of course it's not. I don't give a damn about a dessert."

"Then what is it? What have I done?"

From the way he opened his mouth to speak, Holly expected

him to reply, but instead, he clamped his jaw tightly closed. Then, flicking on his indicators, pulled a quick turn and swerved into a nearby layby where he slammed on the brakes and cut the engine. When he turned and faced her, his eyes were black.

"You're serious? You think I give a toss about a meal? What I'm mad about is the fact that you couldn't even admit I exist to someone who doesn't even matter. They're not friends of yours. They don't live in the same village and in a month and a half, you're never going to see them again."

A sudden heat washed over Holly and tears pricked behind her eyes. There was only one time Giles had spoken to her in a voice like that, and it had ended with her pushing him into the river in Bourton.

"You know why Clarissa couldn't see you. It could get back to Ben."

A tense silence filled the car. Holly's back molars were grinding together. She had no idea where the nearest bus stop was to her, but if he didn't say something soon, she was going to find out. Either that or she was going to walk to Moreton. It wasn't like she had anything better to do with her time.

"I don't care," Giles spoke slowly, his consonants considered and perfectly enunciated. "I don't care who sees us out together. Whether it's Drey or Jamie or your whole flipping antenatal class. Why keep seeing so much of me if you're so embarrassed?"

"That's not fair. You're as much to blame for this as I am. If you hadn't tried to sabotage my business—"

"I'm sorry, okay! How many times can I apologise? What I did to the shop, to us, that is the biggest regret of my life. And I am going to have to live with that forever. Knowing that I lost the best person I ever met and that she's going to spend her life with the wrong guy because I screwed up."

"What?" All the air flew from Holly's lungs, leaving her breathless. This wasn't like the other times Giles had said something like this. The times he had jokingly alluded to what a great couple they would be. Normally, he was just trying to get a rise out of her, but there was not even the slightest hint of jest in his voice.

"Ben and I are happy," Holly said quietly, tears welling as Giles stared at her with an intensity that bored into her soul.

"I don't believe that. Not happy enough, at least. Ben is not what you want. Or need. He is not right for you."

"He is the father of my child."

"That shouldn't be what dictates how the rest of your life goes."

"So you would take on a woman and raise another man's child?"

"No." His word was as blunt as it could be. "I would raise *your* child."

His words were causing her head to swim.

"Why are you doing this now? Why today, after everything I've already had to go through?"

For the first time since they had left the pub, Giles' anger shifted, and a look of deep remorse clouded his expression.

"I'm sorry. I really am for that. My timing is horrendous. But surely you can see he's everything you came to the Cotswolds to get away from?"

"Ben is nothing like Dan," Holly spat. Her hackles rose, and she felt herself shift in the seat, squaring towards him. After all the pain that Dan had put her through, there was no way she was going to let anyone tar Ben with the same brush.

"Oh, he won't cheat on you and he wouldn't turn into a stalker on you either. But he's safe. He's predictable. You stay with Ben, then life will be perfectly comfortable. You and your baby know you'll always have a roof over your head and a nice house with a garden and probably another kid and a dog when the time's right."

It was a future Holly had envisioned more than once, yet hearing the words from Giles' lips just riled her further.

"What's wrong with that? I happen to like dogs."

"What's wrong is that Ben doesn't set your heart on fire. You know he doesn't. You are too amazing to settle for average Holly Berry. You deserve everything. Every ounce of passion and pleasure and excitement the world has to offer."

"The type of excitement I would get from you, you mean?" she said, raising an eyebrow. If he was going to start these things, then he could damn well finish them.

"Be like that if you want. But at least I'm honest with myself about what is going on with us." He had swivelled around in his seat.

"What's that supposed to mean?" she spat. "What do you mean by that?"

"You know exactly what I mean. You know deep down how I feel about you. You... you..." It was like trying to say her name was as bad as spitting venom.

"I what, Giles?" Holly shifted closer and pulled his face towards her. She wanted him to look her straight in her eyes. If he was going to call her out, call out her relationship with Ben, he could at least look at her when he did it. "What do you want from me?"

"What do I want?" Giles' eyes widened with surprise at this comment. "I want you to be truthful. I want us to be truthful."

"You want us to be truthful?"

"I do."

"That's all you want?"

"That's all I want."

"Fine."

And before she could stop herself, their faces were within an inch of one another. Their lips were only an inch apart.

CHAPTER TWENTY-SEVEN

They were so close. So close she could feel his every breath on her skin. The feelings inside her propelling her forward. One more inch and their lips would be touching. She would be kissing Giles. She would be kissing Giles Caverty. That was what he wanted. She could tell that now. That was what he had been waiting for all along.

"Stop!" Her head snapped back away from him. Her heart was hammering in her chest as she struggled to draw breath. "I… I…"

"It's okay…" Giles said softly, reaching out and brushing his hand against her cheek.

"No. It's not. It's not okay." The trembles that had rippled through her body during the moment of near kissing transformed into shaking that afflicted her hands and knees. "How can you say it's okay? We nearly… we could have… I'm having a baby with Ben. I am with Ben."

He was staring at her. His eyes shone with disappointment, and yet all she could think about was his lips. What it would have been like if she'd actually let herself go through with kissing him. Why? Why was her mind doing this to her?

With a final gasp, she turned away and buried her head in her hands.

She couldn't be sure how long she remained there, sobbing into her hands as Giles rubbed her back and made soft, calming noises, but when she sat up, his eyes met hers and were shrouded in guilt.

"I am sorry. I shouldn't have pushed things."

"You think?"

She wanted to add more. She wanted to say that the entire moment was absolutely his fault. That this predicament was of his making only. But she knew it wasn't.

"Look," Giles said, sitting up straighter in his seat. "Let's be honest with each other. It has been a crazily stressful day with you and your dad. And you needed someone. That's all it was. You needed someone there, and I just happened to be present. I'm pretty sure you would have nearly kissed Frank had he been the one here with you after the day you've had."

Holly coughed out a laugh. A mixture of snot and tears dribbled down her face in a way that must have looked truly horrendous, and with no other options available, she wiped her face on the back of her sleeve.

"I'm sorry."

"You have nothing to be sorry for," Giles said, lifting his hand towards her, only to stop and place it back on the steering wheel, his composure returning immediately. "I'll be honest, the whole running nose look, it's utterly unattractive. I don't even know what I was thinking." This time, she managed to raise her lips into the smallest smile. But rather than reciprocating, Giles' face fell. "I think the best thing to do is that I drop you at your car, and we say goodbye. And this time, for good." At his words, Holly felt the tears welling again in her eyes. "It's what you wanted before," Giles continued. "It's what you asked for, and you were right. That's what we should have done. I have been selfish, trying to keep a piece of you when you're not mine to keep. And I'm sorry. So I'm out. I respectfully bow out of a contest I was never invited into. You, Holly Berry, are the most incredible woman I've ever met, and I hope that bank manager knows it."

Even more tears were tumbling down now, accompanied by a throb in her chest. Why was it hurting this badly? Like Giles said, this was what she had asked him for. And it wasn't like they even saw that much of each other. A once a week, half-hour food shop, that was all. This is what was best for all of them. For Ben and the baby. So why did it continue to hurt?

"Come on," he said, reaching across and offering her hand a slight squeeze, before letting go and turning the engine on. "Let's get going."

For the entire journey, her eyes remained fixed on the passing scenery. She couldn't look at Giles. She didn't want him to see how she had lost all control of her tear ducts and become a complete snivelling mess. She also couldn't bear the thought of looking at him and knowing that this really was the last time the pair of them were going to be together like this. It just wasn't right. More than once she was certain she could feel him throwing a glance at her and she was tempted to look back and meet his eyes, just so he could see how hard this was for her too. So maybe he would be able to read all those things she wasn't able to say to him. But what were those things? No. She wouldn't say it, not even to herself. It was ridiculous. It was just the stress, that was all. It was the stress of her dad, and the baby and Ben being away, and if she let those words escape into the air, there would be no way ever to bring them back. So she stared out at the darkening sky and the shadows of the trees and wondered if being an adult was meant to hurt as much as this.

When they reached Moreton, Giles parked up right next to her car.

Before she could get her belt off, he was already around her side of the car, opening the door, and offering a hand to help her down.

"So, this is it," he said. They were standing apart. Too far to reach out and hug each other. Or do anything else, accidentally. "Are you going to be okay to drive home? I've got to go the same way back, so I can follow you back to your turning if you like?"

Rather than refuse, like she normally would, Holly nodded her head.

"Thank you."

"Okay, well than I guess this is it, Berry."

Silence engulfed them. Heart hammering silence that she knew she could end by getting into her car and saying goodbye to it all. Goodbye to him.

"Thank you," she said.

It was his turn simply to nod and remain quiet. "Well, I've got some karma to clear up. If giving up the fight for you isn't worth a clean slate, I don't know what will be." Despite the light tone he tried to add to his voice, neither of them managed to smile.

She wanted one last hug. She wanted to say that she had never wanted to kiss anyone like she wanted to kiss him and that he was the person who she felt most comfortable with. That she didn't feel bad about whinging or laughing about ridiculous things. That she didn't have to feel like everything was perfect. She wanted to tell him so many things, but what she actually said was.

"See you later, Caverty." Then Holly Berry got into her car and drove home.

CHAPTER TWENTY-EIGHT

By the time she reached Bourton, it felt like the whole day had been a dream, from the counselling session to her dad in the hospital. None of it felt real. Or at least like it had happened to someone else. The morning at work felt like it had happened weeks ago, as did Giles turning up to rescue her from the rain in Cirencester. The only thing that felt remotely real was the way she felt in the instant of that near-kiss. *That* she could recall with absolute clarity. It was hormones. She knew it was hormones. And like Giles said, her emotions were so heightened with everything that had happened that day, it was no wonder she was overcome.

Parking up in the front of the house, she took her bag off the passenger seat and debated which house to go into. She had planned to stay at Ben's while he was away. At *theirs,* but now more than ever, she felt a strange uncertainty in treating the place like that. She didn't want tidy organisation. She didn't want clinical white kitchens and pristine cutlery drawers. She switched the key in her hand to the one for Jamie's front door, only to change her mind again a moment later, and open the door to Ben's. After all, this was her future. Hers and her baby's future. This is where she should be.

In the kitchen, she kicked off her shoes and flicked on the kettle, ready to fix a caffeine free tea. Only while she was waiting for it to boil did she take out her phone and realise it had been turned off since the hospital. Upon turning it on, she had seven missed calls, all from Ben, along with a text message from Caroline saying Ben had been trying to get hold of her, and she hoped she was all right. Praying he hadn't got so concerned that he had messaged her mum and dad, she called him back. This time, he answered immediately.

"I am so sorry," he started. "I rang the shop and Caroline told me you'd had to go to the hospital with your dad. Is he okay? Are you okay?"

Starting the conversation with Ben apologising wasn't what she had expected, but then again, she should have known better than to think Ben wouldn't have tracked her down.

"It's been a long day," Holly said honestly.

"I take it you had your phone off at the hospital? You were there for a long time. Is everything okay? Are you back home? Is he going to be okay?"

Holly's mind went into overdrive at the stream of questions.

"I just forgot to turn it back on," she answered the most important part first. "But Dad's doing okay. He was lucky, a minor heart attack. He'll need monitoring, of course, but he should be able to make a full recovery."

"Thank god. I am so sorry I wasn't there for you. You shouldn't have to go through something like that on your own."

An image of Giles picking her up and shielding her with his umbrella flashed through her mind. She tried to quash it.

"It's okay. Honestly, I'm fine."

"And what about the bump? You know you should be

avoiding all types of stress at the minute. Do you think you need to check in with the doctor?"

"The bump is fine, we are both fine." Holly smiled to herself, considering the fact that if every pregnant woman went to visit their doctor whenever they suffered a stressful day, they'd probably be a two year waiting list at most surgeries.

"As long as you're sure. I'm going to speak to work, make sure I'm not sent away again until after the baby is born. It's just not worth risking this."

"You don't have to do that."

"Yes, I do. You and the baby are my responsibility. I need to make sure I step up. If anything were ever to happen before the birth, I wouldn't be able to live with myself."

A wave of nausea swept through her. He was so earnest. So damn truthful. He had done everything she had asked of him since they had got back together, and she had repaid him by what? Nearly kissing a man he despised. From this point on, she was going to be the best damn girlfriend he could ever dream up.

"I love you," she said. "And I know how lucky I am to have you."

"Well, you're going to be stuck with me and my sock folding ways for a good while yet," he said. Even though he wasn't there, Holly lifted her cheeks in a strained smile. "So, I'm getting an early train tomorrow morning, meaning I'll be back in Bourton by three and ready to go to the antenatal class."

And just like that, a feeling of dread settled on Holly.

"I was thinking we should miss it this week," she said. "You know, today has been pretty stressful and you've been away and it would be nice to spend some time together."

Her suggestion was met by silence.

"I know that you're embarrassed by what happened last

week, but honestly, in a couple of months you will see the funny side of it really. And remember, these classes are supposed to help you through the stressful times. If anything, going this week is more important than any other. And if you're worried about me not making it on time, don't be. I'll be back, I promise."

CHAPTER TWENTY-NINE

The minute she got off the phone the guilt flooded her. Why hadn't she said she had gone for food with Giles? If she'd told him he had taken her home from the hospital, he would have understood. Possibly. But then she would have needed to explain why he was there in the first place.

Holly's mind went back and forth as she tried to work out what she was supposed to say. She could tell Ben that she and Giles had met up shopping a couple of times, but what did that achieve? What good would him knowing do? Their counselling sessions had already made her aware he felt like she was holding things back from him. What would this do, other than confirm that? It wasn't worth bringing it up, not when nothing had actually happened with her and Giles.

She stared at her phone, knowing it wasn't going to ping. Ben had already sent his good night message, and her mum had also called with a quick update of how her dad was, and to let her know that they'd be discharging him the following day, as long as his tests were all okay. No, no one was going to message her now. Especially not Giles.

A kick to her ribs jerked her out of her moping.

"You're right, this is a good thing," she said, rubbing her belly and talking to the bump. "It's good that this has ended now. It's a good thing. Because me and your daddy are going to take care of you together. Your daddy's a good man, you know. Very good. Probably too good for your mummy…" She stayed there when another kick, that felt remarkably like a response. It made her laugh. "I know, don't worry, you're going to be well looked after. I promise. And I will tell your daddy about seeing Giles. I will. I just have to work out what to say."

The next day at the shop, things were abnormally quiet. Even when the shop was empty, Drey normally made enough noise to make it feel like the place was full. She would talk to Holly about reality television shows she watched, or places she planned on travelling to at some point. But that Saturday, Drey wasn't in much of a talking mood. Under normal circumstances, Holly wouldn't have minded. She understood everyone needed quiet moments, and not everyone could be upbeat all the time, even Caroline and Drey, but with everything going on in her head, the silence was infuriating. Her thoughts flitted constantly between the near-kiss she shared with Giles and the elation that she felt surge through her, and the devastation she knew it would cause Ben when she told him. And she had to tell him. She had to. Didn't she?

"So, how was your dad about the whole protest thing?" Holly said, needing to be distracted from her own disasters. "You have told him, right?"

Drey was on her knees, sweeping under the shelves. It was a job they almost never got the time to do on a Saturday, but Drey had been working at turbo speed all morning; every jar was filled and every shelf dusted, as if she was also trying to keep herself busy.

"He's had a busy week," Drey replied, not looking at Holly as she spoke.

"Drey! You said you'd tell him."

Huffing characteristically, Drey stood up and turned to face Holly. "Have you told Ben about the fact you've been going on secret dates with Giles Caverty?" She raised her eyebrows. Holly stared at her fixedly.

"They're not dates. They are trips to the supermarket."

"Which you normally only do with someone you're in a relationship with," Drey said.

At that, Holly didn't have a response. She ground her teeth together, before letting out a huff remarkably similar to Drey's.

"We are not talking about me. I am a grown woman, my mistakes are my own. You're not an adult. Hence, I had to drive up to London to get you out of jail last week. And we made a deal. I wouldn't say anything as long as you told him yourself. I don't feel comfortable with him not knowing."

This time Drey's sigh was less teenage, and more like the worry laden exasperation you would get from someone double her age.

"I know, I do. And you know how grateful I am to you and Ben for arranging the lawyer. But I promise it really was a bad week last week. Dad had back-to-back meetings, and then there was this whole thing with my aunt, and the doctor already said he needs to lower his blood pressure. But I promise, I will talk to him."

"Tonight?"

"Well, tonight I'm actually meeting up with Eddy."

"You are not." Holly had never heard herself speak in such a maternal, cross, commanding voice. Drey smirked.

"Wow, calm down there, mother. He's got some things of mine, that's all. Don't worry. I have no intention of giving him the time of day. But you need to clear the air with these things, don't you? He's a dick. I was an idiot for being with him. I just need some closure. And maybe to kick him in the nuts too."

At this, Holly couldn't help but chuckle. She didn't doubt for a second that Drey was capable of taking a grown man down a peg or two.

"Well, tell your dad when you get back, okay? The longer you hold on to these lies, the worse it becomes when you finally have to tell the truth," she said. And as the words left her mouth, she felt like she was speaking as much about herself as Drey.

The closer it got to closing time the more nervous Holly became. The good thing was, with the baby on her bladder, and attempting to knock her pelvis out of place, she had a justifiable reason for constantly going up and down the stairs and looking fidgety. Another good thing with the pregnancy, is that people assumed hormones and tiredness were the reasons for her getting their orders wrong on multiple occasions, not because her head was going simultaneously over all her past and future actions, wondering how the hell she had got herself into such a mess.

Having gone over and over it in her mind, she had decided she would mention her meetings with Giles to Ben before the antenatal class. That way, they might get stuck in a deep conversation and she may even get away with missing the session.

Some silver lining had to come out of this entire mess. Although maybe she would be missing it anyway, currently there was no sign of Ben. She checked her phone, every couple of minutes, waiting for the text to say that he was back in England and would be driving home soon with Georgia—or perhaps would be taking the train and would need picking up from the station, but currently her phone was utterly silent.

It was only as she was turning the sign to closed and reminding Drey again to tell her dad that Holly's phone rang.

"I am so sorry," Ben said. "There was a delay on the Eurostar, and I couldn't get any reception. We've just got into St Pancras."

"Oh, it's fine." Holly glanced at her watch. The class started at seven-fifteen. Driving back from London at the best of times took two hours, and that was assuming he was on the right side of the city. "We really don't need to go."

"Look," Ben said, speaking before she had a chance to say anything else. "Georgia's going to drop me straight at the hall for the classes."

"Don't be silly, you don't want to go straight from work and travelling to sitting on the floor for an hour."

"Yes, that's exactly what I want to do. I'd better go. We need to get the car, but I'll be there, okay? I'll be there."

"Great," Holly said. But it didn't feel great. It didn't feel great at all.

CHAPTER THIRTY

Holly Berry was dressed very nicely. She was wearing make-up and perfume and had even straightened her hair. Not because she was trying to be particularly fancy, but because she had needed something to keep her hands busy. In the hour between getting home and leaving for Cold Aston, she had turned into a veritable nervous wreck. Her first thought had been to go around to Jamie's and hear about how the last week with all of Fin's relatives had gone, but all the lights were off in the house and it was obvious that no one was home.

Stuck with her own company meant stuck with the thoughts going around and around in her head, which mainly consisted of how close she had come to kissing Giles. Even now, if she closed her eyes, she could feel the exact same tension in the air. The static buzzing between the pair of them. If she had just moved an inch forward…

She shook her head and snapped herself out of the moment. This wasn't about Giles. He was officially in the past now. This was about her and Ben, and thankfully, she knew exactly what she was going to say to him. She was going to get straight to the point with an apology. Say how she had no excuse for her behaviour but how she wanted to discuss it at the next counselling session. How she had actually called an end to their meetings, even though they had genuinely been accidental to start with. It had just been the situation with her father that meant he had come to help her. There was no need to tell him about the near-kiss, though. What would she say anyway? That there had been a *moment?* No, nothing happened, and there was no point dredging up things that didn't make any sense. She needed to show Ben that he could trust her. And he could. Giles was out of the picture. He was gone forever. She just hoped that her face didn't display the ache that spread across her chest when she said those final words.

At five to seven, she got into the car and drove to Cold Aston.

Autumn was very much on the turn. The brown leaves on the trees were growing scarcer and scarcer, the crops harvested and replaced with ploughed brown earth. Above the grass verges several red kites swooped and circled on the thermals. As she parked up outside the village hall, she cut the engine.

She had already told Ben that she would wait outside in the car for him; the last thing she wanted to do was to be drawn into a conversation with any of the couples inside. Particularly with Clarissa. No, she would ensure she avoided Clarissa entirely this session. Although knowing Clarissa she had probably already told everyone inside about Holly's false alarm.

She glanced at her watch. Ten past seven. Ben had messaged five minutes ago, to say he was five minutes away, so where was he? Every minute waiting for him was making her sick to the stomach. Maybe this was a good thing. Maybe him turning up late like this was a good enough reason to skip the session.

Just as she was about to pick up her phone and ring, a royal blue Mercedes turned into the church carpark. Before Holly had time to check who was driving, Ben leapt from the passenger seat. In a near sprint, he grabbed his bag from the boot, then waved to the driver, before racing across to her. Her own car door swung open, and before she could even blink, Ben was in the car with her, cupping her face and planting a kiss straight on her lips. It was a long kiss. The type that they had lost themselves in endlessly at the beginning of their relationship, but it was hard for Holly to concentrate on such things now. It felt like it had come out of nowhere to start with. Her body tensed beneath Ben's hands.

"You have no idea how much I have missed you," Ben said when he finally broke away from the kiss. "I am sorry for cutting this fine, but I told you I'd make it."

"Right." Holly forced herself to smile.

"Is your dad okay? Do you need to see him? Is he out of the hospital?"

The bombardments of questions hit her like a wall, as she struggled to remember exactly where she wanted to start this conversation. Still, she tried.

"Ben, I wanted to talk to you about something."

The smile on his face dropped a fraction before he lowered his head. Rather than looking concerned, he looked saddened. His eyes dropped away from her as he nodded his head.

"I know."

"You do?"

"Of course I do. I know I'm not the most emotional person,

but I'm not completely oblivious. I get it. I do. After everything I said about Paris, and there I was. I know that must have been hard on you, given how I reacted before."

The script Holly had planned was slipping further and further away from her, as she scrambled to keep a track of her thoughts.

"There are other things. Other things I need to talk to you about."

"I get it," Ben said. He reached out and took her hands again, only to drop them a moment later and place them on his lap. The action confused Holly. Did he know about Giles? Why would he kiss her, then not want to hold her hands? That didn't make any sense.

"Ben, while you were away—"

"There was a mix-up with the rooms," Ben said, cutting her off.

"Sorry?"

"There was a mix-up in the hotel when we got to Paris. Georgia and I were placed in a double room together on the first night."

"Oh?" Holly wasn't expecting to be the one to be surprised during this conversation, but her eyes widened. "You were?"

"It was only for one night. And I know I should have told you, but I didn't want to cause you any upset. I mean, there was nothing we could do about it. I slept on the floor and the second night they found us another room, and I moved in there."

"Oh," Holly answered again, feeling the dread deepen in her. Ben had told her about having to sleep in the same room as another woman in a situation that was entirely beyond his control, and he looked absolutely devastated. Now she was going to have to tell him she had been meeting a man he hated to do their weekly food shop for months, and there was no justifiable reason that she could give other than insanity.

"I know it was wrong. I should have told you at the time, but I wanted you to know, because, well… you know. It felt wrong, sharing a room with another woman. And added to the whole Paris thing… I didn't know how to bring it up."

"Okay, it's fine." Holly nodded to herself, taking in several deep breaths. She needed to get her part out now. It would be a car confessional. A chance for them both to unburden. This was good. She could do this. "It's fine. It really is. But I need to talk to you about something, too."

A sudden bang stopped her words in their tracks and made Holly jump in her seat. An act that was amazingly uncomfortable in her given state. With her heart racing, it took her a split second to realise where the sound had come from. It hadn't been a bang at all, but a knocking directly behind her on the window. Outside, the soft creased face of Florence, the instructor, was staring at them while she tapped at her watch, seemingly unaware of how she had just given Holly a near heart attack from her surprise.

"Are you ready? We need to get started?" she said. "Everyone else is waiting."

Holly's heart was pounding. She sucked in a breath and forced herself to smile.

"One minute," she said, offering her widest smile at Florence. She nodded before turning back to Ben.

"She's right," Ben said, reaching for the door handle. "We should get inside."

"No, I need to talk to you first." A worried looked crossed Ben's face, before he shook it away and his expression softened.

"I get it. Honestly. I get it. I do. I do. And we will talk about it. We'll talk about it all later, but we need to do this class. This is important."

And before Holly could stop him, he had slipped out of her grasp and was walking towards the hall.

CHAPTER THIRTY-ONE

The good thing about being late in the class was that there was zero time for chatting or the type of niceties that Holly hated. Which also meant that there was zero time for Clarissa to accost them. One hour. That was all she had to get through, Holly thought as she lowered herself to the ground and took the first deep breath of the class. One hour, then they would be back and in the car and she could tell Ben everything. It was just an hour later than planned. She could do this. She would do this.

"Holly?"

"Sorry?"

Ben was looking at her expectantly. "Florence said you need to switch positions. You're going to be sitting on the balls. See?"

Only then did Holly notice that everyone else was on their feet, and their partners had fetched the large bouncing balls from the corner of the room for them to sit upon.

"The gym balls?"

"They're exactly the same as the birthing balls, apparently."

Holly looked at the exercise equipment and the reflections

of all the women in the mirror. Several of them had managed to get on their ball with little to no fuss, but more than one was looking at the item with an expression indicting they were having the exact same thought she was.

"I'm meant to sit on that?" she said, eventually. "What if I fall off?"

"Don't worry, I'll keep you steady," Ben said. "I've been reading about how good these can be. Lots of babies like to be bounced to sleep on them. Come on."

Holly couldn't listen anymore. Having hoisted her off the ground, Ben was fetching their own ball, working out a place they could put it. The movement of the class had resulted in several of the couples switching places, and the last thing she wanted to happen had happened. Right now, Clarissa was settling onto her ball as she looked to Holly and mouthed a hello. Holly's stomach lurched. If she was sitting by her, she would definitely start a conversation, and she just couldn't risk that. She grabbed their ball from Ben's hands.

"There's space over there," she said, squeezing her way to the front corner of the room, right by Florence. "Last thing I want to do is fall on someone."

Generally speaking, she had always hated to be at the front of any class, ever, but it was the only option. When Ben joined her, he looked less than happy.

"There was room at the back, you know," he said.

"I'm sorry. I just struggle to hear what's being said when we're at the back," Holly lied. Whether Ben was convinced, she couldn't tell, but she was safe from Clarissa, and that was what mattered. With a sigh of relief, she sank down onto the ball, only to start a perpetual bouncing motion. While initially unnerving, it didn't take long for her to get used to the soft movements, and find she actually quite liked it.

"I'll get on the internet tonight and order one," Ben replied, rubbing her back in the manner that Florence had instructed them to do. "It might be quite good for you, after the baby is born too," he added. "You know, help you build your fitness back up."

Holly was only half listening now. In her head she was mentally counting down the minutes until they could leave, acting on Florence's instructions only when she noticed what other people were doing. She occasionally gave non-committal grunts as responses to Ben, hoping he would mistake her lack of engagement with him as concentration on the lesson.

Minute by minute the session ticked by, though as the session drew to a close, Holly realised a new issue had arisen. Sitting at the front of the class to keep out of Clarissa's way had seemed like a great idea when they had got the balls. But now she and Ben had a gauntlet to run to get out of the hall at the end. Which came about far quicker than she expected.

"Okay, mums and dads, that was a really great session today. Really great. If you can all return your balls to the back of the room, that would be fantastic. And if you have any questions, I'm here to chat."

Florence was smiling at them all, her eyes full of warmth, and it took Holly a second to realise what she had said. One by one, people clambered to their feet. Several couples had already clustered together, holding their balls between them, blocking the route between Holly and the exit.

"We need to get out," Holly muttered.

"Are you all right?" Ben squeezed her shoulder lightly from behind. "Is everything okay? This isn't about what I told you before, is it?"

Holly could hardly even think straight enough to figure out

what he was on about. All she knew was that she had to get out of there now.

"No... I'm just, just a bit hot, that's all."

"Woohoo! Ben. Holly!"

Holly's heart sank as Clarissa waved her arms like she was calling across an entire football pitch. Desperate to make herself invisible, Holly lowered her gaze, and shuffled forward as if she hadn't heard.

"Please, can we just leave?" she said to Ben. His eyes narrowed on her for less than a second before he nodded.

"Okay, we can go." He had picked up the ball, and attempted to return it to its rightful place, but each path he turned, people were chatting, blocking his way.

"Just push your way through," Holly hissed at him.

"I'm not going to push a load of pregnant women while I'm holding a giant ball. I'm pretty sure I can get arrested for that," Ben said. Holly's throat tightened. Clarissa was moving towards her. Her sights locked on the pair of them, Floyd dragging his heels slowly behind. Any moment now, she would reach them.

Holly's patience snapped.

"Give me the ball," she said, and snatched it out of his hands.

Had she seen a video to view herself, she suspected she looked like one of those round based wobble dolls she could remember from her childhood, where you could knock them down but they would bounce back up again. But she didn't care about that. All she wanted was to get out of the hall. She twisted her way past the first cluster of people, and past another couple who were talking to Florence. She was nearly there. She was nearly free to go. The only thing blocking her way was a couple deep in conversation.

"Excuse me," she said, using a voice that was well above the average volume for the room. "Sorry, can I just get past?" The pair continued talking. It didn't look like a pleasant conversation, judging from their scowling, and had it been any other situation, Holly would have let them be, but she needed to put this damn ball away. For a split second she considered dumping it and running, but she had no doubt that Ben's eyes were on her and he would never leave a place without putting things away properly.

Rigid with frustration, Holly tried shuffling to the right, only to find all the racks on that side already filled. And Clarissa was encroaching. Any moment and she would be on them, wanting to tell them about some new baby spa she had discovered and discuss the pub that Holly had been to with Giles.

There was nothing else she could do.

Holly had never been in any of the school netball teams. She had tried out for the basketball team, and had quite enjoyed it, but genetics weren't on her side, and being five foot two meant she was never destined for a long-term career in the sport. Besides, she had got the job at the sweetshop and would have struggled with any weekend commitments. Still, at that moment, she thought back to all those lessons in the school gym. Those endless drills of bouncing and dribbling and passing to one another, and most of all, shooting.

She would only get one shot at this. She knew that. One shot to land the massive birthing ball in the hoop. Then it would be a clear run out of here and to the relative freedom of telling Ben about Giles. Lifting her arms above her head, she set her sights on the top corner ring and angled herself accordingly. If it had been the school netball try-outs, Holly had no doubt that she would have been handed the position of goal shooter on the spot. It was beautiful. The ball rose and fell in a perfect arc, with barely a wobble before it settled into position. Slightly disappointed that no one saw to congratulate her, she turned around, filled with smug satisfaction, only for it to disappear in an instant.

The people had dispersed dramatically, having moved to various places around the room, and there were Clarissa and Ben. Together. Deep in conversation. Blood rushed from Holly's cheeks as she hurried towards them. How much could really be said in that time? Her legs shook beneath her as she struggled to walk. How long could they have been talking for? Less than a minute.

Half gasping, half panting, she slipped in between the pair, hooking her arm into Ben's. Immediately, she could feel the tension radiating from him.

"Is everything okay?" she said, louder than she anticipated. Her voice sounded fake. Overly jovial. Clarissa was smiling, though. So they couldn't have said anything too much, could they? Ben was probably just tense because she had mentioned the incident from the previous week and knew how much Holly didn't want to talk about it. "What are you two nattering about?"

"Oh, nothing much," Clarissa said, her smile almost as big as Holly's. "I was just saying it was a shame we didn't get to catch up at the pub."

Ben's lips moved slightly, but no sound came, until a moment later, when he was looking at Holly.

"Clarissa was saying how good I looked in pink," he said.

"I did," Clarissa beamed. "I mean, a pink polo shirt looks good on most men, don't you think? But I didn't even recognise Ben in it. He should definitely wear that colour more often."

CHAPTER THIRTY-TWO

The temperature in the hall was suddenly sweltering. Holly fanned her face with her hand, trying to cool herself down. Was she sweating? It felt like she was sweating. She was certain she could feel beads of perspiration forming on her neck. Ben's eyes were still locked on her. Waiting for her to say something. But what did he expect her to say here, with Clarissa hanging on their every word?

"We should really get going," Holly said, trying to yank Ben by the arm. "It's been a busy couple of days."

"Of course, you've been on your feet all day," Clarissa smiled, flashing her perfectly gleaming teeth. "I don't envy you at all. Really, I don't. But we will have to catch up. Head back to the Pickle and Fig, together this time?"

"Yep, sure," Holly said over her shoulder as she began walking away. She had dropped Ben's arm after the yanking did nothing. But he was at least following behind her. She could feel him. His silent presence shadowed her out of the hall and into the chilly evening air. She needed to say something. At some point, she had to say something. But what?

What could she say? Only when she pinged the lock on the car did Ben move a little faster as he opened up the passenger side door. Slowly, Holly followed suit on the driver's side. She closed the door and placed her hands on the steering wheel, but made no attempt to start the engine. They were doing this now. They were having this conversation now. And she was terrified.

"Pink shirt?" The first words came out of Ben's mouth with so much force they made Holly jump. "Pink shirts. I guess I don't need too many guesses to know who you were out with last night, then."

"I was going to tell you," Holly began. "I wanted to tell you, straight away, but Florence was at the window. And then there were all the things you were saying about Georgia."

"This is not the same," he snapped, his voice as close to a shout as Holly could remember him ever doing. "What happened with Georgia was an accident. I didn't ask to sleep in the same room as her. Can you tell me you just turned up at the pub and he was there?"

"No, that's not what I'm saying. Yesterday was hard, Ben. Seeing my dad in a hospital bed like that. I didn't want to be alone. I needed someone there. Jamie and Caroline and everyone was busy, and I just needed someone."

"You needed him?" The question was direct, but Holly couldn't bring herself to answer it. It felt like a trap. "Is this the first time you've seen him?" Ben questioned. "Is this the first time this has happened? The first time you two have been alone like that."

This wasn't right. She had planned everything she was going to say. How she was going to tell the truth. How she was going to say that the friendship just continued after she found out she was pregnant, but she didn't want to hurt Ben and knew he would be upset she had kept it a secret. She had everything worded, ready to go. So why couldn't she find those words now?

"Holly?" Ben pressed. She gulped down a lungful of air, wishing she could lie. It wasn't too late to say this was a one-off thing, but then she couldn't lie to him. Not telling him had been one thing, but lying entirely, she just couldn't do it.

"Yes. Yes, it's the first time we've been out. But we have bumped into each other now and then. That's all."

"Bumped into each other. What does that mean?"

The air in the car wasn't getting any cooler, and the heat seemed to have travelled all the way down to her feet. Were hot feet a sign of something she worried momentarily, before refocusing on the situation.

"I've seen him at the supermarket," she said truthfully. "He does his shopping at the same time. He sometimes helps me carry the bags back to the car."

Ben's expression was as icy. "Like I offered to come along to do? How often?"

Her voice warbled, and she pressed her lips together, fighting the tears that were trying to escape, but no actual sound came out.

"How often has he helped you? Is this a once or twice thing? Or is this something you and him do every week?"

There was no stopping the tears now. They tumbled down her cheeks in great torrents, as she tried to even her staggering breaths. But it was no use. When she finally spoke, her voice came out as a near whisper. "Every week. Every week since I discovered I was pregnant."

"Jesus Christ, Holly," Ben dropped his head into his hands. "Six months. You've been seeing him behind my back for six months?"

Her throat was clamped shut now. Blocked by all the tears rising from her chest.

"I'm not seeing him. It really was an accident to start with. Then he just kept coming along. I promise I wanted to tell you."

"Oh, and let me guess, there just wasn't a right time? What with you staying at my house every other night? Or I don't know… how about the counselling sessions you made me go to, because you were concerned I wasn't being open enough in this relationship. God, you two must have been laughing behind my back the whole time."

"It wasn't like that," Holly insisted. "I swear."

"Then what was it like?" he said. "Make me understand. Explain to me why you did this?"

Outside, people were reversing out of the car park. She stared at the glowing lights for a minute as she tried to figure out what she could say. *What was it like?* What was spending her time with Giles like? It was like a breath of fresh air; she wanted to say. It was a chance when she could just relax. When she didn't have to feel like she was invading Jamie and Fin's privacy if she stayed there, or worry that she was being too messy, or too lazy or not thinking about the baby's health with every meal when she was at Ben's. It was the one time she felt like she had no responsibility other than to be herself.

"Are you sleeping with him?" Ben said.

The question came out of nowhere and felt like an arrow through the heart.

"What? No. Nothing like that."

"Nothing at all?"

Holly opened her mouth to assure him, but hesitated. That was all the time it took for Ben to get his next question out.

"Would you be with me if it wasn't for the baby?" he asked. The anger and disbelief had gone from his face now. As had the volume in his voice. His words were low and quiet and caused the hair on the back of her arms to rise. He looked squarely at Holly. "Would you?"

Holly sucked in a breath. "There's no point doing this. Dr Ellis said that. She said it's pointless going over things like this. The fact is, I don't know. Just like I have no idea whether you'd be with me if I hadn't got pregnant. This is a pointless conversation."

She was about to turn on the ignition when Ben mumbled something under his breath.

"What was that?" Holly said.

She turned her head back to him, expecting him to be looking at her. But he kept his head facing his lap.

"I think it's time we admit the truth. There is no trust in this relationship. I don't know if there ever has been. This whole thing has been flawed from the start."

"Flawed from the start? What's that meant to mean?" She hated it when he did this. When he beat around the bush, rather than coming out and saying exactly what he meant. "What do you mean by *flawed from the start?*"

When Ben looked at her this time, the hardness and sadness had faded from his eyes. Instead, all that remained was deep resignation.

"This relationship is over. That's what I mean. This relationship is over."

CHAPTER THIRTY-THREE

They didn't exchange a single word on the car journey back to Bourton. Several times Holly glanced to her side, but Ben's face was fixed away from her, his eyes locked on outside the car.

Her body felt hollow and numb. Not racked with pain like it had been after she and Giles had nearly kissed, and certainly not twisted with guilt. But there was a similarity to how things felt. The finality that had come with both actions. This wasn't some argument they could talk through with the counsellor. No amount of fiery make up sex was going to set this right at the end of the day. She and Ben were officially over. For good this time. She could feel it in her bones. As she stopped at the junction in Bourton, the baby turned in her stomach, causing her to gasp.

Ben's attention snapped back to her. "Is everything all right?"

She nodded. "It's fine. We're fine." As she finished turning, she placed her hand on her belly, feeling its rotations within her.

Not kicking. No anger, just a shifting of position. Just the same as she was going to have to do.

"If you could put my things together, that would be great," Holly said. The silence may have already been broken, but that didn't make it any easier to speak. "If you don't mind. Or I can come around at some point tomorrow and pick everything up when you're out."

"Is that what this has come to now? Switching places in and out of the house, not even speaking to each other?"

"I'm just trying to make life easier for you. For both of us," Holly stressed, but she could see that Ben wasn't believing any of it. "I think we should try to make an appointment with Dr Ellis as soon as possible," she continued. "Work out how we can make this work when the baby comes along."

"Uh-huh." Ben grunted. They had reached the stage of grunts. She ground her teeth together, trying not to get irked by the response.

"Is that a yes?" she said. "Do you want me to make an appointment this week?"

"Whatever you want."

"Well, will you turn up if I make the appointment? That's what I want to know," Holly finally snapped, before sinking back into the car seat. "I'm sorry. I don't want to rush you. I know this can't be easy. I just want to get things sorted, that's all."

If she was honest, it surprised her at how matter of fact she was being. Perhaps it was the baby. The hormones. Nesting. Wasn't that what they called it when the woman suddenly kicked up a gear and got ready for the baby's arrival? Of course, for most people, that included buying new bed sheets, and cute cuddly toys and cleaning out the kitchen cupboard of all the ancient jam jars and pickles that were stored at the back collecting dust. For Holly, it meant getting her life sorted, so she knew how her baby was going to be looked after and whether she actually had a roof over her head.

As they pulled into the driveway, a list a hundred points long was whirring around her mind. A list she really needed Ben to be on board discussing, but all those thoughts were pushed to the side as she pulled up outside the house.

Her heart fluttered and sank simultaneously at the sight of Jamie's van parked on the driveway. Jamie was home. On the plus side, it meant that she wasn't going to be on her own tonight. Having Jamie and Fin there to talk to would be good. It just meant she was going to have to admit her failings a little sooner than planned, that was all. Holly hadn't even cut the engine when Jamie's front door flew open.

It wasn't unusual for Jamie to open her front door for Holly and Ben when they got home. She often checked in with them about their day, particularly when she had been gone for a while, and thought they might slip into Ben's house without seeing her, but there was something different about this moment. The urgency with which she had swept outside. Maybe they were expecting her to arrive with the baby.

Holly recalled a message sent early in the day, which Holly had forgotten to reply to. Was it possible that Jamie had taken her lack of response to mean she was off having a baby? Possibly. Particularly if Ben had been unreachable in France too.

Yet when Holly and Ben stepped out of the car, Jamie didn't look to the back seat for any signs of a baby carrier. Instead, Fin came and joined her, wrapping his arms around her, almost as if to pin Jamie down. She was practically bouncing on her feet.

"Do you have any idea how late you guys are? I've been expecting you to come home like half an hour ago. Where have you been?"

"Actually, we—"

"Scrap that. I don't care now. You're here now. That's what matters. You're here and I can't wait any longer. Look. Look at what happened."

Holly wasn't entirely sure where, or what, she was supposed to be looking at, until Jamie stretched out her hand. There, on the ring finger of her left hand, a massive diamond haloed by a dozen smaller ones was glittering in the muted evening light.

"Fin asked me to marry him!" Jamie said, leaping across to Holly and pinching her in a tight squeeze. "Isn't it amazing? He asked me to marry him! Obviously I said yes."

She was beaming. Glowing in a way Holly couldn't remember ever seeing before. And she was happy for her. She was so happy for her. Jamie deserved all the love in the world and so much more. And she was about to say as much when Ben spoke across her.

"I guess that's just perfect timing," he said.

CHAPTER THIRTY-FOUR

People who say they couldn't tell the difference between caffeinated and decaffeinated tea were liars, Holly decided. She had known this from the first time she had a decaffeinated cup after she discovered she was pregnant and now, what had to be two hundred cups later, she was just as certain. But it was late in the evening and after all the adrenaline rushes the baby had dealt with over the last forty-eight hours, she didn't feel right giving it anymore. And so she spooned another heap of sugar into the imposter tea, hoping to make it slightly more palatable.

"I'm sure it's not over, over," Jamie said, sinking down into the chair opposite Holly. Her ring really was impossibly impressive, even for someone like Holly who knew nothing about jewellery at all. She had tried steering the conversation back to the proposal, particularly as Jamie had bought a bottle of bubbly to share when they got home. But the drink now sat unopened on the edge of the table. "You guys have broken up before. Several times if I recall."

"We have," Holly agreed. "But this time it's over. Properly

over. He won't forgive me for meeting up with Giles. Even if it was just to do the food shopping each week. And deep down, I understand. I get it. Really, I do."

"You seem awfully okay about it?" Jamie eyed her sceptically. "Should I be worried that the breakdown is imminent?"

"Probably," Holly admitted. "I don't know. It's so strange. I just feel like the last few months we've been so swept up in the baby that there's been no time to think about us. To think about what I want."

At this, Jamie chewed down on her bottom lip and avoided Holly's eyes.

"What? What is it?" Holly asked.

"Well, that sounds like you were just stringing him along to me, if I'm honest."

"What?"

"Well, this whole thing with Giles. Why? Why would you do that? You know how much of a creep he is. Honestly, I don't blame Ben for flipping his lid. I'm surprised he didn't commit you to a bloody asylum. You know that man tried to ruin your business, don't you?"

"I do. I do. I know everything you're going to say to me, because I've said it to myself a thousand times, but it doesn't matter, anyway. There was never anything other than friendship between us."

"Friendship that led to you nearly kissing."

Holly may have neglected some details of hers and Giles' meetings to Ben, but she had told Jamie everything. Including how he said he wanted to be with her. And the fact that they had very nearly kissed.

"That only happened under the extremely stressful situation of seeing my dad in the hospital. And nothing technically happened," Holly countered, although she could see Jamie was having none of it.

"But you can't really believe Giles is genuine? You know he's been trying to get one over on Ben for years."

Holly pushed back her tea. "You're saying he's spent the last six months trawling around a supermarket, packing my bags and loading things into the car, being there for me, just to get one over on Ben?"

"I wouldn't put it past him."

"You don't know him."

"I knew him a long time before you." Jamie let out an exasperated sigh. "Honestly, I hope all this is down to hormones."

"He has changed."

"Leopards and spots, springs to mind."

The pair fell into stony silence. It was clear the two of them were just going around in circles, but Holly didn't know how to stop it. She felt bad for defending Giles when Ben was the one who had ended up so hurt, but it was Holly who hurt him. No one else.

"I'm sorry," Jamie said, reaching out her hands and taking Holly's. "I am. I guess I'm disappointed, you know. This morning I imagined us, our little families, growing up in adjoining houses. Baby Ben and Holly toddling down the aisle at our wedding."

"I get it," Holly said. "You're not the only one who's disappointed by this."

That was it, she realised. That was the exact way she felt. Disappointed. Not grief-filled, or angry, but disappointed. This relationship and baby with Ben had been a chance to have that future she had always dreamed of, stable and loving. And one with certainty. But now she doubted if any relationship could offer her that. Then again, maybe it wasn't the relationship that was the problem. Maybe it was time she admitted she was the issue.

"So, I hate to do this to you for the second time, but Fin's arranged an engagement party. He'd already told his British Nana he was proposing months ago, and she was so overly excited. The party is mainly family, on both sides. None of his American side can make it at short notice, obviously, but we were really hoping that you guys would come. His Nana wants to meet my friends, you know. So does my mum. She's heard so much about you."

Holly took a deep breath in. Last time Jamie had held a party, it had been for her birthday. That night had resulted in Ben finding out about her being pregnant, along with a trip to A&E. It had also been the night she reconnected with Giles. She didn't know whether to laugh or cry thinking about it now.

"It's fine," she said. "In a few weeks, Ben and I are going to have to be on speaking terms again, for the baby's sake. We might as well start now."

"Thank you," Jamie said, reaching out and squeezing Holly with yet another hug. "Any chance you can make sure there's no drama this time?"

"I will do my best."

CHAPTER THIRTY-FIVE

The first few days after breaking up with Ben, Holly was a mixed bag of emotions. Not having her dad in the shop meant that she was having to stretch the hours of both Caroline and Drey, although she was trying to take up as much of the slack as possible. No doubt her doctor and midwife wouldn't approve of all that time on her feet, but she was grateful for how it kept her distracted. After all, it was tough to think about how disastrous her life was, when she was weighing out two hundred grams of white mice and watching children squeal with delight at marzipan badgers.

In a telephone conversation with her parents on the Tuesday, her dad had made it abundantly clear that he was coming back to work as soon as the doctor gave him the all clear. He also stressed several times that there was absolutely no need to hire anybody else for her maternity leave. Despite his optimism, Holly wasn't a hundred percent convinced and placed an advert in the window for *possible part-time work*. Hopefully, her dad would never need to know, but even if he found out, he could hardly be mad at her for covering all her bases.

What surprised her most, though, was how much she had enjoyed being in the house with Fin and Jamie in the evening. Her expectations of house sharing with a newly engaged couple was that it would involve constant displays of affections and sickly sweet pet names. That was certainly how it had been at the very start of their relationship when Fin had just moved in. But now, it was different. Yes, they were affectionate, but in an incredibly unobtrusive manner. Fin made Holly several candles to help with her relaxation and was all geared up to teach the little one to skateboard as soon as it was old enough to walk.

"I can't believe you've gone this long and not found out what the sex is," Jamie said on the Wednesday evening as they sat on the sofa sharing a large pizza. "I don't know how you're not bursting with excitement. I'm bursting with excitement. There's no way I'd be able to wait when it's our turn."

"Well, you won't be able to avoid it, anyway. Not with my Nana."

"Your Nana?" Holly asked.

"Yup, she has a way. She knows. Every time one of my cousins has been pregnant, she's guessed the sex, and she's got it right. Without fail. She says it's something about the way you're walking or carrying or something like that."

"Well, if you don't want to know, you better stay away from her tomorrow night," Jamie said.

Tomorrow night, Holly thought with a sinking feeling in her gut. The engagement party had come around scarily quickly. Probably because Holly had tried to keep every thought of it pushed right to the very back of her mind.

"Is she going to be there?" Holly asked.

"Yup, his Nana, and his aunts and uncles, and his sixteen cousins."

"Sixteen?" Holly gasped. She was an only child, and so were

her parents. She was sibling-less and cousin-less. Although her face obviously showed her surprise.

"There aren't that many," Fin replied, poking Jamie playfully. "I've got nine cousins here and four more in the States."

"And their husbands and wives."

"That's true. And Clem messaged today. Asked if she could bring a guy too."

"Clem?" Holly asked.

"My second youngest cousin," Fin clarified. "She's an artist. She and I were destined to be eternally single, but I guess that's changed now."

"Great, so loads of happy couples." Holly didn't mean to sound so despondent. The moment the words left her lips, she looked apologetically at her friends. "I'm sorry, guys. I didn't mean it like that. I really didn't. And I know Caroline is coming on her own. She won't let Michael attend after he announced the pregnancy at your birthday."

"Poor Michael," Fin responded, although his eyes glinted with a smile. Jamie's sense of humour had definitely rubbed off on him, and it showed. Plus, he hadn't mentioned Holly's energy channels for at least a month.

"Honestly, I'm sure Ben and I can coordinate, so we don't need to be there together," Holly said. Her messages from Ben were still almost monosyllabic, but he was replying to her, and that was something. Then again, they would need to speak at the counselling appointment on Friday, anyway. Assuming he was going to turn up.

"Have you thought more about what you're going to do when the baby arrives? You know the offer of changing rooms is still there. But we should probably get it all kitted out ready. Just in case the little one arrives early."

Holly nodded in agreement. That was another sad thing

about this relationship bust-up. When she and Ben had been together, it was so much easier. They would have lived at his. The baby would have its own room, decked out with things that Jess and Caroline had passed on, like a feeding chair and the baby's bouncing seat. She couldn't just go in there and take everything. That would be churlish, but that meant she was going to have to spend a fortune on all those things again.

"You don't need to worry about me," Holly said, realising that, once again, the conversation had turned to her, despite the fact that Jamie and Fin had more than enough excitement of their own to be dealing with her. "You guys need to be concentrating on you. Have you any idea when the wedding will be?"

At her question, Jamie and Fin exchanged a look, implying this question had been discussed many times before.

"I want a short engagement," Jamie spoke first. "I hate these engagements that go on for years and years."

"As do I," Fin took over speaking. "But I've got friends all around the world that are going to require some coordination. And family. I know they're going to need a fair bit of warning to get over here."

"So basically, I don't get my way," Jamie said with a smirk.

Her comment elicited a raised eyebrow from Fin, who then drew her in close for a kiss.

"Well, how about I spend the rest of your life making sure you get your way with everything else?"

She huffed in mock annoyance.

"You know, I am absolutely holding you to that."

"I would be disappointed if you didn't. Besides, you know Nana said she'd pay for the whole thing."

"Yes, I am absolutely not letting that happen," Jamie replied.

"We'll see."

Now, looking at the pair of them and how they fed off one another's energy, it seemed impossible that Holly had ever thought they were mismatched. They were a perfect couple. The way they were so happy. And how they could compromise without anyone feeling like they had lost out. The thought filled her with a sad nostalgia for her relationship with Ben. They had been so close. So close and yet miles away.

At the shop the next day, Caroline assured her multiple times that, firstly, she would definitely come to the party without Michael. And secondly, she would drive, so there wasn't even the chance of her getting drunk and making a scene the way her husband had previously done.

"I will have to speak to Ben, you know. Spend some time with him. He's one of our oldest friends. I can't blank him—particularly given the fact that—" She stopped abruptly.

"What?" Holly said. "Go on. You can say it. Particularly given that I'm the one to blame in the whole relationship breakdown."

"I didn't say that."

"No, but you thought it."

Caroline remained silent as she placed a jar of sweets back on the shelf, then straightened up several boxes of fudge.

"I just can't get my head around it. I really can't. Giles Caverty. It makes no sense at all. I mean, I get the man is charming and has a lot of positive physical attributes. But after everything he did."

"I know, I understand. I get it. But you haven't seen Giles. He's changed. He really is trying to make amends for it. He was there for me."

At this point, Caroline let out a sigh.

"I mean, the fact he drove to come and get you in Moreton, then took you to the hospital to see your dad, is something. I'm pretty sure that's more good deeds in one afternoon than the man has done in the rest of his life. Although he cancelled it out when he tried to kiss you, of course."

Holly's stomach squirmed at the comment. When she had told Caroline she and Giles had nearly kissed, Caroline, like Jamie, jumped to the same conclusion that it must have been Giles that instigated the moment. But every time one of them brought it up, she found herself back at that moment in his car—the heat burning through her, heart hammering, desperate to feel his lips press against hers.

"Well, Giles isn't something we have to worry about," she said. "He's gone. That chapter of my life is definitely one hundred percent closed. Again."

With the sweets now straightened, Caroline returned to the counter, giving Holly a stern look.

"Just don't go into labour tomorrow, will you? It would be nice to have a night out without any drama."

"I will definitely try not to," Holly promised.

CHAPTER THIRTY-SIX

Now that she was closing in on her due date, Holly Berry officially loved her baby bump. It was difficult to believe, given the journey it had taken to get her there. There had been a couple of months early on when the swelling of her abdomen simply looked like she had enjoyed a few too many of her own sweets in the shop, but that wasn't the case anymore. Now, she had a wonderfully neat, round bump, and as strange as it may have sounded, she had never had so much fun dressing up and showing off her figure. Perhaps it was the fact that she was soon to be without it. And so she was going to make the most of it. Like most things, Caroline had gifted her a dozen maternity dresses, all flowing and loose, that accentuated her figure beautifully. She tended not to wear them at work, choosing the elastic waist trousers instead. But this was Jamie's engagement party, and she was going to look good.

The shop had been abnormally quiet the entire day of the party, so Holly had shut half an hour earlier than usual to give her a little more time to have a nice bath and do her hair. Not that she did much. Just washed and blow-dried it. Still, when

Caroline beeped her horn outside, Holly felt better than she had done in months. With a slick of lip gloss and a spritz of perfume, she was ready.

"You look nice," Caroline said when Holly manoeuvred herself into the car. "Is this a ploy to make Ben see what he's missing out on?"

"No," Holly said honestly. She'd been trying to forget that he was going to be there. "I just wanted to look nice for me, that's all."

Caroline smiled back at her. "Well, you do. And I'm glad I got all the baby sick out of that dress before I gave it to you. It looks really good."

The engagement party was taking place at a hotel restaurant near Stroud. It wasn't a part of the Cotswolds Holly went to often, although, with the rolling hills, open space of the common, and views that stretched out for miles around, it certainly wasn't a location to be sniffed at.

"Apparently, all Fin's family are staying at the hotel," Holly said. "He booked out all the available rooms for them."

"Of course he did," Caroline replied. "Although I'm amazed he managed to get any space."

"Apparently, he booked the place six months ago."

"Six months? They'd only just got together."

"Yup. And he'd already decided that he would propose to her by this weekend. I can't decide if that's amazingly sweet or just a bit creepy."

"It's Fin. It was probably something to do with the stars, meaning this was the best possible weekend to propose."

Holly chuckled. "Can you imagine what the wedding is going to be like? You know, there will probably be loads of famous skateboarders there. We should brush up on their names so we know who we're talking to. Although, I'll be honest, watching re-runs of the X-games so that I might know someone at a wedding seems like a bit too much effort. Besides, I'm probably not going to have much time on my hands," Holly said, patting her bump.

"Just you wait. Late night TV was a saviour, my best friend."

When they turned off the main road, and into the restaurant car park, they were greeted by a wall of red. Autumn colours set the whole building alight. Crimson and orange ivy crawled upwards against the front facade, matched by the vibrant colours of the trees. Meanwhile, the sky desperately tried to cling to the last of the autumn sun, and not a single cloud tarnished the pale blue sky.

"Wow, of course, they got a perfect evening for it," Caroline said. "Which is good because it means you can always come outside. If you need a bit of space."

Holly nodded. She had already spotted Ben's car parked on the other side of the car park. There was going to be no avoiding it. No time to find her bearings before he arrived.

"Don't worry," Caroline said, squeezing her hand. "I'm here for you. Obviously, I'm here for him, too, so if I tell you to shut up and go away at any point, you know I'm just being fair with my friendship."

Holly laughed, though her laughter was short lived. Her attention had once again fallen on the trees ahead of her. So many amazing colours, yet many of the leaves had already fallen to the ground below. It was the same with the ivy. As she continued to study the foliage around the restaurant a thick lump formed in the base of her throat, which rose quickly, until a single tear leaked down her cheek.

"Hey, it's alright," Caroline said, reaching over to wipe away the stray tears. "It's going to be fine. I promise you. Ben wouldn't make a scene at Jamie's big day. It was only a joke, I don't have to talk to Ben that much if it's going to upset you."

Sniffing back as many tears as she could, Holly shook her head.

"No it's not that… it's not about Ben."

"Then what is it about?"

Holly tried to speak again, but the tears were rolling fast now.

"Hols, what is it? Talk to me."

Still sobbing, Holly clenched her fists, trying to stem the flow, but there was no stopping it. Every time she glanced out the window it started again. Her breaths were uneven and shallow. More a gulping of air than actual breathing. "It's… it's… it's the trees."

"The trees?" Caroline questioned. "You have some memory about the trees?"

Holly shook her head again, hastily trying to wipe away the mixture of tears, foundation and mascara that now coated her face in a sodden mess. "No. No, it's just… they're dying you know. All the trees are dying." Now she had said the words out loud the pain in her chest exploded as the sobbing reached an entirely new level. "The trees are dying."

Next to her, Caroline steepled her fingers and pressed them against her lip, before letting out a low hum. "I think this might be something to do with hormones, don't you?" she said quietly. "It can do funny things to you. Once I burst into tears because the butter melted. And it was on my toast at the time. And another time when I was stopped at a red light…"

Holly wasn't listening. Whatever Caroline was saying, it didn't matter. Not in the grand scheme of things. At that moment, all that mattered was these beautiful trees and their red and orange leaves fluttering to the ground.

"It's just so unfair," she said, cutting across whatever anecdote Caroline was trying to give her. "They're so beautiful. All of them. And it doesn't even make any difference how old they are. Do you know that? It's not just the old trees that die. It's the young ones too. Mummies, daddies, baby trees even. They die too. The baby trees die too."

Next to her, Caroline was doing her best to suppress a laugh. Taking a second to wipe back the tears of her own. "I did know that, yes. But honey, I promise you, this is not as big a deal as you think. It's just hormones. Trees don't really have mums and dads. Besides, this happens every year. And it's not like the trees actual die. It's only the leaves."

"That's even worse," Holly said, emitting an almost wail like cry. "The trees have to watch as all their leaves fall off and die in front of them. They grow them. They grow these leaves from these tiny little buds. They nurture them and then, just like that —" she paused to snap her fingers, "—gone."

It was almost more than she could bear. All those leaves lost to the ground. Separated from their tree for all eternity.

From the driver's seat, Caroline reached across, and rested her hand on her Holly's cheek, before pulling it around gently, so that they were facing one another. Using her thumb, she wiped the patches of skin beneath Holly's eyes before moving on to wiping her cheeks. Holly had stemmed the crying now, having reduced it to a mild snivelling. Still, she couldn't look out the window, or even attempt to speak. Fortunately, Caroline knew exactly what needed to be said in that moment. With the smile still twitching at the corners of her lips, she sat back in her seat.

"I think maybe we should check your make-up before we head inside."

CHAPTER THIRTY-SEVEN

Thankfully for Holly, Caroline kept a small make-up bag in the car. There wasn't much in it, but then Holly didn't really wear that much make-up, and the most important item proved to be the wet wipes, which she used to scrub at the black mascara stains that weaved their way in tracks down to her chin.

"You have to admit, it is sad," Holly said as she used some concealer to try and patch up the blotchy red patches that had formed from all the crying.

"It is very sad, but we're not going to get into it again," Caroline replied, no longer bothering to hide her smirking. "Besides, we need to get in there. People are going to think we're avoiding the party if we stay out here any longer."

With a final glance in the mirror, Holly pinched her cheeks and forced herself to smile, before turning back to Caroline.

"You're right. Let's do this."

A concierge was waiting inside the doorway, ready to take their coats. He dipped his chin slightly as he smiled at them both.

"Ladies, can I assume you are here for the engagement party?"

"We are," Holly replied, wondering what the wedding was going to be like if this was just the engagement party.

"Excellent. Pre-dinner drinks are taking place in the drawing room. Down the corridor. You'll see the door open on the left."

As they walked along the wood-panelled corridor Holly's thoughts were finally distracted from the periodic death of trees and drifted instead to Giles. He had taken her to a place like this on their first date, the very same day they met. Of course, it wasn't an actual date. It was a fake date. A chance for him to get to know as much about the shop as he could and use it against her. But it had felt real. The way they spoke so easily to one another. That hadn't changed, even if so many other things had.

"Deep breath," Caroline said, giving Holly's hand one last squeeze before she stepped into the room.

At a rough guess, there were fifty people of varying ages, from children sitting at a table, shouting at one another as they played with toy cars and a game of Uno, to the more elderly ladies and gentlemen that Holly assumed were Fin and Jamie's grandparents, nursing glasses of sherry. Origami birds had been placed on the tables; the same sort that Fin had made to decorate the room during Jamie's birthday party, yet Holly's eyes were drawn to the lone figure by the bar, dressed impeccably in his shirt and tie. A year ago, Holly would have wondered if he'd come straight from the bank looking like that, but now she knew that the shirt he was wearing, with its light check, was one of his casual ones, and the red and green socks that peeked out below his trousers, were a lively upgrade from the plain black or blue ones he always wore to work. This was social Ben.

"Right, you need to find someone to talk to," Caroline said, now two steps in front of Holly in the room. "I'm going to the bar to say hi to Ben. Spreading the friendship, remember?"

"Right," Holly said, forcing herself to sound optimistic.

"And don't talk to anyone about the trees okay. And stay away from the windows. Just in case."

"I will."

And just like that, she was on her own.

It wasn't the first time she had been on her own at a party. When she'd worked in London, Dan hated attending any sort of work do. Even Christmas parties. So she had always gone along without a date. But those were work parties, and she had known most of the people there, even if she usually didn't socialise with them. This party was entirely different. Maybe she should introduce herself to someone, she thought. Alternatively, she could head over to the kids' table. She played a mean game of Uno, after all. No, a toilet break would be the best thing, she quickly decided. A long toilet break, by which time Caroline might be finished talking to Ben and be free to hang around with her instead.

However, no sooner had Holly had the thought she was accosted by a very tall woman in skinny black jeans paired with a vibrant yellow poncho.

"Holly!" The woman leaned in and kissed her on both cheeks. "I can't believe I'm only just meeting you. Now, tell me, how are you doing? Jamie said the morning sickness was pretty terrible there for a while."

It took only a second before Holly saw the similarities between this woman and her housemate. There was no doubt who she was talking to.

"You must be Sandra," Holly said, finding this woman's

infectious smile very similar to her daughter's. "So pleased to meet you. Jamie's said so much about you."

"And I'm sure it's all terrible," she laughed.

"Not at all." Holly released a deep sigh of relief. Jamie constantly commented on her mother, particularly how relaxed and cool she was. Having at least one other person she could talk to made her feel much more at ease.

"So, tell me, and I want the truth. What do you think of my new son-in-law to be? He's quite *alternative.*" Holly chuckled at the manner in which Sandra stressed the word, alternative, but Sandra wasn't finished yet. "Of course, I'm not surprised Jamie would end up with a man like that. A lawyer or teacher would just be too ordinary. But tell me, do we like him?"

The conspiratorial, *we,* only enamoured Holly even more to Sandra. She had expected the night to be awful, but already she could feel her cheeks aching with a smile.

"We do," she said. "I will admit he took a while to get used to, but we like him now. We like him very much indeed."

"And he will be good to my daughter?"

"I think the fact that he booked this place two months after they started dating says something about that, don't you?"

"That's true. Now, help me out. I'm trying to work out who all these other people are. I thought his family was American."

For the next ten minutes, Holly and Sandra giggled away in the corner of the room as they tried to identify the various people from Fin's side of the party. His grandmother, they decided, was the elderly woman wearing an obscene number of diamond rings that must have cost more than the average house, while Holly assumed that the people similar in age to her were the cousins. She couldn't recall any names or what they did. However, with the waiter continuing to fill up her glass of sparkling grape juice, it didn't take long for a toilet break to stop becoming a getaway ploy and become a genuine need.

"I'm sorry, I'm just going to have to pop to the ladies' room," she said, resting her hand on Sandra's arm lightly. "I'm sure we will be sitting down for food soon."

"I hope so," Sandra replied. "I will talk to them about this. All this wine and no food. It's like they want to get us drunk. They need to make sure there are plenty of nibbles available at the wedding."

"I will make them both aware of your request," Holly laughed, then headed towards the door.

She was just in the doorway when the voice cut through her.

"Can we talk?" Her stomach flipped, performing a complete somersault. Given how much Holly had wanted to spend the night avoiding Ben entirely, she had assumed he would feel the same. Apparently, that wasn't the case. Inhaling slowly, she turned around to face him.

Never had she noticed how big and wide his eyes were before that moment, Holly thought as she was forced to look straight into them. In that second, she could imagine exactly what he looked like as a child. All floppy hair and big brown eyes—like butter wouldn't melt. Would her child inherit those eyes? She didn't want to think about that right now.

"Hi," she said, her voice still constricted by the knots in her stomach.

"I realise I have been rather distant this last week," Ben said, glancing down at his feet. "And I know we've got our session together tomorrow. I just wondered if we could talk before then. You know, get on the same page about what we are both going to say."

Wasn't the whole point of the counselling sessions that they described how they truly felt at that moment without any rehearsals? Holly wanted to say. But she didn't. It was clear that this was painful for him.

"I don't think this is the most appropriate time," Holly said, then added quickly. "But yes, we can talk. Perhaps in the morning."

"Or I could drive you home tonight. I know you came here with Caroline. Maybe we could talk if I give you a lift back, then?"

In terms of successful car conversations, Holly had experienced exactly zero this last week, and she didn't think tonight would fare any better.

"I think tomorrow would be better," she said. "I'm going to head off pretty early, and I know Jamie would like it if at least one of us stayed later."

He nodded. "Okay, tomorrow. I could walk you to work, maybe?"

"I'll message you in the morning," Holly said. Then, feeling like the conversation had been amazingly amicable and that this would be a good place to end, she turned back to head to the toilet when she was hit by a cascade of people. It took her a second to find someone in the crowd she knew.

"What's going on?" she said when Jamie appeared next to her. "Are we going through to dinner?"

"No, it's Clem."

"Clem?" The name rang a bell, though Holly couldn't for the life of her think what that was.

"Fin's cousin. Everyone's clambering to get a first look at this date of hers. Apparently, she's been talking about him for nearly a year, but no one actually believed he was real. Anyway, they're about to turn up, so she messaged the cousins. Fin said she craves being the centre of attention, so I guess she's the one who I need to watch at the wedding. She will probably turn up in a white dress, too."

Holly wasn't sure whether it was a joke or not, but from the smile stretching on Jamie's face, she wasn't going to let something like an attention-seeking relative ruin her day.

"Come on. Let's see what they're like. Apparently, she met him at an art gallery opening. I mean, I already know he's an idiot, don't you?"

Somehow swept up in the moment, Holly followed Jamie and the small crowd of Fin's giggling relatives to the main entrance. There was, Holly thought, something special about being part of a family like this. A massive group of people who had each other's backs—even if they were mocking Clem at that precise moment. It was a shame it wouldn't be like that for her child. The thought resulted in a pang of sadness. She had found it near impossible to find a man who wanted to settle down with her and build a future before all this. Who on earth was going to want to raise another man's child with her?

"Wow, that must be them pulling up now."

Her attention was drawn away from her melancholy to the car that had just driven up the driveway. The cousins were straining their necks, trying to get a proper look at the couple as they exited the vehicle. At that moment, a wave of bile stung the back of Holly's throat, and her knees began to tremble. Holly knew she didn't need to look any longer. She knew exactly who drove a car like that.

CHAPTER THIRTY-EIGHT

"You know he ghosted her for months."

"I thought he'd moved abroad."

"I heard he'd got engaged."

Holly felt sick. Nausea was so intense that it was actually making her dizzy. And it didn't help that the baby had taken this moment to practice taekwondo on her kidneys. Around her, the excited gabble continued.

"Does anyone actually know what his name is?" One of the cousins asked.

"Giles." Holly's voice was a half-croak, half-whisper. Yet several pairs of eyes turned in her direction. "His name is Giles. Giles Caverty."

Any hope she had had that her memory was playing a trick on her or that the vintage sports car he had picked her up in on that first date was, in fact, incredibly common, evaporated the instant he stepped out of the vehicle.

"Hols?" Jamie's hand was on her shoulder. She could feel her there but couldn't draw her eyes away from the scene. Giles, moved around to the passenger side to open the door for his date. Clem? Was that her name? Giles and Clem. They sounded like a couple. Holly watched on, still glued to the pair, as Giles kissed Clem gently on the lips before closing the door behind her and walking towards the entrance. Walking towards them.

In an instant, Holly shook her body and turned back to Jamie. "Well, this is unexpected, isn't it?" she said. Holly knew she was smiling. She had definitely made herself smile. Her cheeks throbbed from it. But a prickling heat was burning behind her eyes.

"We should head back in," Jamie said. "They're going to call us for the meal any minute. And Mum has said how she wants to sit next to you. She said you really hit it off."

Holly wanted to follow Jamie. She tried to shrug off this feeling of drowning clamped around her lungs, fix her smile back in place, and spend the rest of the evening laughing with Sandra about all the mischief Jamie had gotten up to as a child. But she couldn't move. Her feet were rooted to the spot like heavy weights had fixed to the soles of her shoes. Several of the cousins had gone to greet Clem and introduce themselves to this mystery man, who was shaking hands with them all, smiling widely, with his arm wrapped tightly around Clem's waist.

"Come on. We already knew what Giles was like, and this just confirmed it. I'll kick him out myself now. There's no way he's ruining this for me."

Holly felt her chin drop in a nod, but no sooner had Jamie's hand dropped from her shoulder than Giles' eyes had moved from greeting various relatives and were fixed on her. She watched the colour drain from his cheeks—the smile drop from his face. Then, a second later, he left Clem with her relatives and marched towards Jamie.

"I am so sorry. I had no idea. Clem said it was her cousin's engagement party. That's all I knew. I'm sorry. She said he was American, but I didn't know he had proposed. I am so sorry. I'll make my excuses and go now."

Jamie dipped her chin in a nod.

"Well, that was easier than I thought it would be," she said.

He nodded quickly before his eyes moved to Holly.

"I'm sorry," he said. "I didn't mean…."

The tears were now burning the back of her throat, yet somehow she kept them in check. That didn't mean she could move, though. She still couldn't move. But more surprising than that was the glaze glistening Giles' eyes, too.

"Can we talk?" he said, looking solely at hers.

"I think you've caused enough trouble in Holly's life again. Don't you?"

Giles tilted his head with a confused look. "What did you tell them?" he said.

Now the tears were burning her throat so much that she couldn't even form a word.

"Giles, honey, can we go inside? My grandmother is desperate to meet you."

Considering they were cousins, not siblings, Clem and Fin looked surprisingly similar with their surfer locks and tall stature. In Clem, that equated to legs that went on for miles protruding from her belt-length skirt. There were no similarities between Holly and this woman at all. And it was tough to believe Giles had ever found her attractive when this type of woman was throwing herself at him.

Despite Clem's comment, Giles' eyes remained locked on Holly for a second longer before he turned his attention to his date.

"I am so sorry. I've just had a message from work. An entire contract is about to go down the pan. I've got to go."

Her face fell, and Holly felt a pang of guilt for the girl, not to mention a deeper twinge of disgust at the ease at which Giles lied to her.

"I thought you didn't have to work today?"

"I'm sorry. I really am. I thought my staff was capable of doing this by themselves."

With a pout that wouldn't have been out of place on a runway, Clem inhaled with such force Holly heard the sucking sound.

"Okay, well, how long will it take you to sort it? Fin's parties always go on all night. Maybe you could come back again?"

"I've got to get up to London," Giles said, the lies tripping off his tongue flawlessly. "I think I'll probably just stay the night at that flat there."

Holly watched as Clem's patience disappeared. She didn't know why she was still standing there—still watching them. Had she been a decent person, she would have backed away and given the pair the privacy they needed to discuss the situation, and she was just about to do that when, with a massive huff, Clem stormed passed and headed back into the restaurant.

"I can't believe I actually thought you had changed," she yelled, waving her hands as she went.

With the gaggle of relatives following Clem, the only three people that remained outside were Jamie, Holly, and Giles. It would have been an awkward trio at any time, but this wasn't any time. This was Jamie's engagement party.

"You need to go inside," Holly said, turning to her. "People will start wondering where you are."

"I'm not leaving until I see his car driving off the property."

Jamie fixed Giles with her most venomous glare. Holly had to admit she was impressed. She had seen stronger men crumple at that glare.

"It's fine. I'll make sure he's gone. He's not staying," Holly said.

CHAPTER THIRTY-NINE

Jamie didn't want to leave her. Holly could tell. She could hear the cogs whirring in her friend's head. Jamie wanted to give all the reasons why it was a bad idea for Holly to talk to Giles on her own. And Holly understood. She felt exactly the same way herself. But Holly needed to speak to him. She needed to.

"If you're not back inside in ten minutes, I'm coming to get you," Jamie said. "And I'll be calling the police and telling them he's harassing you. After his track record, it wouldn't be far off."

Holly nodded, but she didn't reply. In fact, she didn't say anything at all until she and Giles were utterly alone. Silence eddied around them, and while the dizziness may have passed, it had left Holly feeling light-headed and less than secure on her feet. Wordlessly, Giles took a single step towards her.

"Don't," she spat, lifting her hand to stop him in his tracks.

"Holly, I'm so sorry. You need to understand—"

"Oh, I understand. I understand perfectly well. Everything you said about changing. Turning over a new leaf was bullshit. You're the same snake you've always been, and I'm the same complete idiot who fell for it. Who thought you could be something more than some deceitful arse. What were you hoping to get from me this time? You can't still be after the shop. Or was it just to humiliate me?"

"Hold on," Giles' guilty expression shifted to something with deeper annoyance. "Don't you dare. Don't you dare say I was stringing you along. You were the one practically living with another man. The one who is about to have *his* baby."

"At least I was honest."

"Oh, well, that makes it okay, then. You can string people along as long as you're honest while you're doing it."

"I wasn't stringing you along. We were friends."

"It was never just friendship for me. And don't pretend you didn't know that."

Holly's fists were clenched by her side. Currently, the bump was calm, obviously asleep in her belly, but if her adrenaline kept rising, she knew it wouldn't take much more to wake it up. Was she stringing him along? More than friendship? How many times had he commented that Holly was his worst idea of a woman and that what they had was and always would be platonic?

"I'm done here," she said, but as she turned around to return to the party, Giles grabbed her by the wrist.

It wasn't a hard grip, but it was tight enough to shock her into stopping. When she turned around, Giles' face was only inches away from hers. His lips were so close she could feel his breath upon her. So close that one slight move, and she could be kissing him. A week ago, she wanted to. But now she wanted to slap him instead.

"Let go of me," she hissed. Her eyes locked on his. The intensity in the meeting of their gaze only stoked the fire that burned within her. Yet his fingers remained on her wrist. The pressure of his touch seared through her. "Get your hands off me," she repeated.

This time Giles let her go. He bowed his head for a fraction of a second before he lifted his gaze back up.

"What did you tell Ben?" he asked quietly. "What did you tell him about us?"

Part of her didn't want to reply. He didn't deserve to know a thing about her. Any guilt she had felt about the way they ended had disappeared the minute he turned up here.

"What do you think I told him? I told him it all."

"Even… you know… the moment."

Holly sniffed. It was dismissive and bitter and stung the back of her throat.

"I told Ben about our meetings. About the supermarket shops. And you'll be happy to know that he doesn't trust me at all. And now, because of you and your manipulative ways, I barely have a speaking relationship with my baby's father anymore. So if your plan was to turn up here and make sure you ruined my life completely, congratulations, you've done it."

"You and Ben are over? Truthfully?"

At this news, a spark lit up Giles' eyes for the first time since he had seen her at the party. He was practically beaming at this knowledge, and it made her sick to the stomach.

"This is all it ever was to you, wasn't it? A game. Another way to get one up on Ben and me. Some twisted revenge over the shop. Was that your plan all along?"

"No, you can't believe that. You know exactly how I feel about you."

"Yes, so intently, so deeply, that you are another girl's date to an engagement party less than a week after you profess your love for me."

Giles' face hardened. "You were the one who didn't want a relationship."

"And you were the one who said you would do anything for me."

"I would. You know I would. I love you, Holly Berry—"

"Don't. Don't you dare. Your words mean nothing to me. You need to leave."

"I love you. I love you, and I want to be with you. And if you're honest, you want to be with me, too. I was there, remember? I felt it. You wanted to kiss me just as much as I wanted to kiss you."

"We are not doing this. You need to go."

"I don't believe that's what you want. I think you want me to stay. Please, Holly. Let's talk about this properly."

He stepped forward and reached for her hand, which hung limply by her side, but a voice cut across him before he could touch her.

"I think she asked you to leave."

Both of them craned their necks for a better view of the speaker.

"Ben!" Holly exclaimed.

CHAPTER FORTY

"So, you two have had an eventful week, by all accounts. Tell me, how are you feeling now? Ben, why don't you go first?"

The previously spacious office of Dr Ellis now felt claustrophobic. For the first time since they had begun their sessions, Holly and Ben were sitting on separate sofas, about as far apart from one another as they could get in the space.

Thankfully, Giles and Holly's scene hadn't ruined Jamie and Fin's night. Ben was the only one who heard everything that was said. And following his intervention, Giles had indeed left without further comment. Following that, Ben refused to engage with Holly for the rest of the evening. Absolute silence. He hadn't replied to Holly's text messages the following morning either, no matter how many times Holly apologised for what he had heard. Not that it was her fault. In fact, she hadn't even been sure he would show up for their appointment.

In response to Dr Ellis' question, Ben drew in a long, deep breath.

"I think Holly has deliberately sabotaged our relationship because she never wanted to be having a baby with me, and that, deep down, she is probably relieved that this has happened now."

His anger elicited a wide-eyed response from Dr Ellis, who quickly jotted something down on her tablet before turning to Holly.

"Holly, do you agree with that? Do you think you have deliberately been sabotaging your relationship with Ben?"

"No. Of course not. I tried to do everything to get this relationship to work. I was the one who suggested that we attend these meetings. That was all my idea."

"It was. I recall that. So if you were so intent on saving this relationship, why do you think it is you have been seeing this man behind Ben's back?"

"I wasn't seeing him. We would just do our food shopping together. That's all." At this, Ben let out a long sigh, which irrationally irked Holly at a rapid speed. "What do you want me to say, Ben? We were weighing out peppers and talking. That's all we were doing."

"Apart from the fact that he is in love with you. I heard him say it himself, or have you forgotten?"

"You're the one who says I shouldn't believe a word he says. But now you're telling me I should believe that he loves me. I don't know what you want from me, Ben."

"The truth, Holly. That's all I've ever wanted from you. I want the truth. Honestly, most of the time, I don't know if I should laugh or cry." Ben then directed his attention to Dr Ellis. "You know she got annoyed with me for setting up a group chat to look after her? She was really cross about that, yet she's carrying on behind my back."

"I haven't been carrying on anything." Holly could hear how far her volume had risen, but he wasn't listening. What was it going to take for him to listen to her?

"Okay, I think we all need to take a step back from this," Dr Ellis cut in before she could speak again. "Emotions are understandably high. So let me ask you both the same question. What would your ideal outcome be? When you think of your ideal future, what does that look like? I want you both to think about that."

It was certainly a change in direction from the rest of the session, but Holly was on board to try whatever Dr Ellis suggested. With a deep breath in, she closed her eyes and allowed an image to form in her mind. A future of laughter and more children. Of holidays abroad and working in the shop with the baby strapped to her chest. She was still seeing it vividly in her mind when Ben spoke.

"I don't need to think about it. I know. It's me and Holly and our family. It's family barbecues and Christmases in matching pyjamas. It's having all our friends and family present at our twenty-fifth wedding anniversary. Teaching our grandchildren to work behind the till at the sweetshop."

When Holly looked at him, she was surprised to find him staring straight at her with nothing but hope and compassion in his eyes. Her heart stirred.

"That sounds beautiful," she said truthfully.

"And what about you, Holly? Is that the same future you see for yourself?"

Ben's image floated around in her mind. With added moments, too, like her baking the children's birthday cakes in the kitchen, picking them up from the school run, tidying up their toys, and joining the PTA where she and the other parents could whinge about school dinners. She could see so much of it, but there was one thing or rather one person, that wasn't in her image.

"Holly, is that what you see, too? Is that your ideal future?"

So much of her wanted to reply yes. After all, it was the future she had dreamed of for years when she was with Dan. That was the future she had imagined for herself. And he had offered her that, but she had turned it down. She had turned it down because moving to Bourton had changed her. It had made her want more from life. It didn't matter if the man was Dan or Ben. That was a future she no longer saw for herself.

She could feel Dr Ellis' eyes boring into her, but it was to Ben that she turned her head to face.

"I want adventure," she said. "I want to travel. I want to put this baby in a rucksack and spend a month island hopping around Thailand."

At this admission, Ben snorted. "That's not real life, Holly. That's a student's dream. We have commitments. You have a business to run."

"I know that. I do. And maybe it isn't possible, but I want adventures in my life. I don't want them to stop."

"Okay, then we can book holidays. I get good annual leave from the bank."

Holly pressed her lips together.

"Holly," Dr Ellis prompted. "Would that be enough? Would what Ben has suggested be enough? Can you see that future working for the both of you?"

Holly remembered those initial months when she and Ben couldn't keep their hands off one another. When Ben picked her up from work had been the part of the day, she looked forward to the most. But she had seen other parts of him since then. Things had been said that couldn't be unsaid. Things that had caused her heart to shift.

"I used to be able to," she said.

Everything remained in the unspoken words. Holly glanced at her watch. There were less than two minutes left of the session, and, generally speaking, Dr Ellis finished bang on time. As such, Holly reached down and grabbed her bag, only to stop part way as Ben cleared his throat.

"Actually, I have something else to say, if that's okay?"

"Of course, Ben. This is a safe space. You know that."

He nodded, steeling himself with a deep breath.

"Okay, I think Holly needs to grow the hell up."

"What?" Holly promptly dropped her bag back onto the floor.

"I think you need to grow up. You have everything. And it's never enough. That's what I've come to see with you. Whenever things are going well, you don't want to know. You find an excuse to turn it all around and screw it up."

"How dare you! Things haven't been going well, Ben. You've been deluded. For every week I've felt like we could make this work, I've spent another two wondering if we're insane. Feeling under so much pressure to be this perfect person to meet your expectations."

"That's not what you've been saying in these sessions."

"Perhaps that's because I didn't want to hurt you."

"Well, I think it's safe to say you've failed miserably at that."

Holly wanted another retort. She wanted to spit words back at him, but she had nothing else that she could say. With her jaw clenched tight, she dug her fingernails into the sofa's seat.

On the desk, a shrill alarm buzzed, marking the end of their session. She could feel the fury radiating from Ben, and she was pretty sure he was feeling the same from her.

"Okay, I'm sorry, we've come to the end of our time," Dr Ellis said, closing the cover on her tablet. "But I think you'd both agree, we've got plenty to unpack next week. Should I book you in for a double session?"

CHAPTER FORTY-ONE

Holly didn't go back to work after the disastrous therapy session. There was no way she could stick to Agnes' rule of not bringing her bad mood into the shop the way she was feeling. As it was, she'd had to sit in her car for ten minutes just to calm down enough to drive.

She didn't run away. She had never run away. Apart from that single time, Dan cheated on her, in which case she was utterly within her rights. The fact that Ben could say that about her showed how little he really knew her.

Half-moon divots formed on her palms as her nails dug in as she clenched her fists. The hardest part was that Ben wasn't wrong, not entirely. In a couple of weeks, she would have a baby. Those plans she'd had of seeing the world when she'd been free and single now felt out of reach for her. How on earth was it ever going to happen now? But then, maybe it was just the possibility of adventure that she craved. Perhaps it was some kind of reverse nesting.

Rather than taking the turning for Bourton, Holly kept driving straight and headed to Northleach to see her parents.

They had been in constant contact since Arthur's heart attack. Holly had been worried about being too overbearing and had tried to find the balance between supporting her mother and giving them the space they both needed to adjust to their new form of normal, whatever that may look like. As such, this was her first actual home visit. And it was a home she barely recognised.

Much to Holly's disappointment, the homemade cakes and biscuits that usually sat on the table, awaiting visitors, had been exchanged for a large fruit bowl filled with apples and bananas and a bunch of sorry-looking grapes that were already dropping on to the table.

"The doctor says your dad can go back to work next week," Wendy said as Arthur placed a cup of tea in front of Holly. "Of course, I've told him he's only allowed to go in if he promises me he won't stuff his face with sweets—none of that clotted cream fudge, no coconut ice. And no lunch time trips to the bakery either. I will be packing him a salad to take each day."

"Don't worry. I'll make sure he follows the doctor's orders," Holly promised her.

"Good. And I've got him started on an exercise plan too. He's going to make sure he gets his ten thousand steps daily. I've already ordered him one of those fit watch things to keep track of that."

"You'll have a spy camera following me around at this rate," Arthur laughed as he leaned over and kissed Wendy on the top of the head.

"Come to think of it, that's not a bad idea. Perhaps I should start saving up for one. Do you think you can get one online?" Her laughter rattled in her throat. Despite all the smiles, it was obvious to Holly how worried her mother had been. The colour was only just returning to her cheeks, and the trauma of the recent event appeared to have aged her by nearly a decade.

"You don't need to fuss about me," Arthur said. "I'm going to be bouncing on trampolines and jumping into ball pits with the little one in no time. Just you wait and see."

The change in her parents was more than just the fruit bowl. Usually, her Dad would sit on the sofa while the pair of them nattered away in the kitchen. But, other than when Arthur had made the tea, the pair had been sitting right up next to each other at the kitchen table the entire time, and although Holly couldn't see it, she was fairly sure that they were touching knees under the table, too.

"So, tell me, are you all ready?" her mother said. "You know you were three weeks early. Did I tell you that? You should be ready for that. Tell Ben to get your go bag ready."

"And he should put some snacks in there for himself too," Arthur piped up. "Still remember that. Bloody starving I was when I was waiting for you to arrive."

Holly smiled. She deliberately hadn't mentioned anything that had gone on between her and Ben and wasn't intending on doing so. Unfortunately, her mother was exceptionally skilled at reading her.

"What is it?" she said. "Don't tell me you and Ben have had another bust-up?"

Holly took a deep breath in. She was tempted to lie. Say it was just another argument. It wouldn't be the first time she had come to her mother after arguing with Ben. But lying was lying, and no matter how well-meaning her intentions were, she didn't want to go down that route. And they would find out, eventually. She just wished there was a way for her to tell them without causing them more stress.

"I think it's fair to say that this was more than just an argument," Holly said, then continued hastily. "But we still had our counselling session today, which is good. We talked through a lot. We are still very much committed to doing what is best for this baby and raising it together. And I think we'll do that well. I know we'll do that well. Ben's a good guy. Just not the right guy for me. At the minute."

She clamped her mouth shut to avoid her typical habit of babbling when she was nervous. Instead, she remained silent and waited for her mum's response, which took a fair while longer to get to than expected. First, Wendy exchanged a look with Arthur. A long look in which Holly felt her stomach twist and tighten. Before she spoke, Wendy took a deep breath in.

"Obviously, it's not the situation that any of us wanted, but it's better it happened now than further down the line."

Holly waited for more to come. For a lecture on how all relationships require work now and then. Or how they might feel different once the baby arrived, but none of it came.

"Now," Wendy said, standing up. "Do you want to stay for dinner? I'm doing poached fish and steamed veg."

CHAPTER FORTY-TWO

When the alarm rang on Saturday morning, Holly couldn't think of anything worse than having to drag herself out of bed. Rain was pattering on the window, and the wind was whipping the trees so that the branches knocked against the glass. She didn't need to open the curtains to know that it was a miserable day, and something internally reflected that.

As she hoisted herself out of bed, she wondered if her body had finally reached its limit. Every muscle ached. Her arms and knees throbbed, and her back felt like she had just completed three triathlons back to back. The constant flickers of pain across her abdomen were like her body was repelling all this endless stress. Her jaw clicked as she scrunched her eyes closed with a yawn. She had lost count of how many times she had got up in the night for the toilet. It felt close to a hundred, though, in truth, she knew it was probably closer to seven or eight. Hopefully, it would be preparation for all the sleepless nights that were to come.

Downstairs, Fin already had a cup of tea waiting for her.

"I was going to start moving all our clothes and swap our rooms over this morning if you're all right with that?" he said. "You know, given the current situation and everything."

At the start of Holly's pregnancy, Fin and Jamie had offered to swap bedrooms, so there was enough room for Holly to have the baby's crib in with her, but given that she and Ben had reconciled, there hadn't been the need for that. But now he was right. It didn't make sense for her to have the smaller room if she stayed there.

"I don't want you to feel like you have to," Holly said.

"We don't. We just want you to have options, that's all."

After offering Fin her most grateful smile, Holly turned to Jamie. "Have you spoken to Ben recently?" she asked.

"Only briefly yesterday. He said he was going to London this morning. I think he said he was staying overnight."

"He did?"

"I think he was going to spend the weekend catching up with that lawyer friend. He didn't tell you?"

"I must have forgotten." Holly tried to keep her voice casual, but it was tough, given the spasms that cut across her stomach in annoyance.

She got it. She understood Ben was upset, but not even telling her he was going when the baby was only weeks away was just irresponsible. And he'd had the audacity to call her immature.

"Don't worry. We're all here if you need us," Jamie said, reading her thoughts.

Holly smiled in response, although the wind continued to howl both inside and outside.

Even more, the pressurised feeling of the day intensified

when Drey messaged to say she would be an hour late. Given that she had not called in sick once in over a year, it was difficult to feel upset, but with her dad still off and the baby behaving like it was part of an Olympic gymnastics squad, the timing couldn't have been any worse.

"Why don't you just keep the shop closed today?" Fin suggested. "It's miserable outside. I can't imagine you're going to be that busy."

"You'd think, but if the bus tours are already scheduled, then days like this are the busiest of all. People come in to shelter from the rain, buying extra sweets to cheer themselves up."

"Well, if that's the case, why don't I come and help you? I'm sure it wouldn't take me long to get the hang of things."

It was a lovely offer, but Holly knew from experience that having someone in the shop who didn't know what they were doing was much more work than having no one else there.

"Maybe if I'm struggling at midday, I can call you?" she said, trying to make it sound like a compromise before adding. "I'm sure it will be fine, though. Drey said she would be in by ten."

"As long as you're sure?"

"Trust me. I'll be fine."

Despite holding out faith that her young employee would arrive in good time, Holly had barely parked up when Drey messaged again to say she would be even later than she had initially thought.

"Perfect," Holly said as she saw the first bus full of tourists enter the car park. This was going to be a long morning.

Before falling pregnant, a busy shop had made the day go fast. Hours would whizz by, with barely a second to think while she was reaching up and fetching one jar then another, weighing them out and ringing them through the till ready to skip across the floor and do it all again. But it was safe to say Holly's skipping days were on a sabbatical.

She had started positively enough. Moving at a rather impressive speed as she stretched up for the various jars. But then, several customers had wanted sweets from the lower shelves, which were decidedly trickier to get to than the higher ones, given the position of her bump. She was just reaching down for the Pontefract cakes when a searing pain shot down her side. She gasped, dropping the jar as she reached for her waist.

"Are you okay?" The customer asked. "Here, let me grab those." They reached for the jar that had thankfully bounced rather than shattered when it hit the wooden floor. Holly manoeuvred herself up to standing, her hand still pressed on her side. The feeling had been so sharp. So intense. Yet now it was gone. She took a moment, stretched out a little as she shifted her weight from one foot to the other, then looked at the customer.

"Sorry. I got a very wriggly one here that likes playing football with my kidneys."

The customer, who was a woman in her late forties, nodded knowingly.

"Tell me about it. Those last few weeks are the worst. I remember with all three of mine. It was impossible to get comfortable. Ever. How long have you got to go?"

"I'm thirty-seven weeks," Holly said, although sometimes, it felt like she'd been pregnant for at least three times longer than that.

"Could be any day now," the woman said, following Holly over to the counter with the jar of Pontefract cakes in her hand.

"I've heard that most first babies are late," Holly said in

response, parroting something Clarissa had said at their antenatal classes. "So I've probably got a bit of time to go yet."

"Well, just make sure you're prepared. I thought the same with my Beatrix. She came at thirty-seven weeks to the day."

Holly frowned as her side began to throb again, though it was much less painful this time. No doubt the angle she had been at before had made it worse.

"Was it one hundred grams you wanted, or two?" she said, diverting the conversation away from baby talk and back to the lady's sweet selection. Ten minutes later, the shop was empty, and Holly opened her thermos flask to take a long, well-deserved sip from her tea for the first time all day.

She had several text messages from her father, checking whether she was okay and asking whether he could just pop in for an hour, but there was still nothing from Drey. Soon it was approaching midday. Concern stirred in Holly. Maybe she should give her a ring or a text message to check she was okay. If Drey couldn't come in at all, then Holly really wished she could have called to say that. She could always have taken Fin up on his offer of help. Once again, the shop was filling up.

Half an hour later, as the queue gradually disappeared, Holly prayed for the moment when the shop would empty, and she could run upstairs and grab herself a seat. She was well aware that it was her fault for not having one down there permanently, but she had been stubborn about it. After all, the stairs had provided an adequate resting place up until now, but maybe it was time to admit defeat. After all, there were still three weeks to go.

Finally, after what felt like an hour of non-stop customers, a calm fell over the shop. Checking that no one was about to come in, Holly didn't even bother wasting time shutting the door as she waddled up the stairs as fast as she could. As it happened, though, she moved a little too fast.

It wasn't the first stabbing pain she'd ever had from taking these stairs too quickly, particularly when she was carrying bags of sweets at the beginning of the pregnancy, but they never left her gasping like this. Dropping onto her knees, she rested her hands on the top of the landing, wishing she'd taken the time to close the door after all. If someone came in now, the bell wouldn't ring to alert her, and the last thing she wanted was someone catching her in this less-than-flattering angle.

As she took one deep breath in and then another, it didn't take long for the pain to lessen.

With a large exhale, she pushed herself up onto her feet and moved to the storeroom, where she considered picking up the seat. It was a light stool, and she had probably picked it up a hundred times in the last couple of months alone, but she was still having trouble gathering her breath from the last stabbing pain.

"Don't be ridiculous," she said to herself, reaching down to pick it up again.

She paused, the stool hovering in her hands as she anticipated a repetition of that pain in her side. When it didn't come, she headed back downstairs, taking it slowly, resting her hand on the bannister as she went.

When she reached the bottom and turned into the shop, she was surprised to find a figure standing directly at the till.

"I'm sorry," Holly said, dropping the stool and pushing it into the corner. "I was just upstairs. Can I help you?"

When the man turned to face her, Holly didn't think she knew him, he certainly wasn't a regular in the shop, but he did look vaguely familiar. It was only when he spoke that she recalled exactly who he was. And a world of dread filled the air around.

"You can help me by telling me what the hell you think you were playing at?"

CHAPTER FORTY-THREE

She had only seen Drey's father from a distance a couple of times. He had attended the charity fundraiser before Christmas when Holly had raised money for the Weeping Willows Care Home, but she hadn't had a real chance to speak to him then. Most recently, they had conversed over the phone. It hadn't been a particularly pleasant conversation then. But this… this was going to be a whole lot worse.

"Mr Abbot," Holly said, trying to swallow back the lump that had wedged its way up her throat. "This is a surprise."

"I bet it is. What the hell do you think you're playing at?"

The shooting pain started again on her side, this time accompanied by a short kick. Apparently, this was a very uncomfortable position for the baby too.

"Is everything okay with Drey? Does this have to do with why she is so late today?" she asked, hoping to sound casual.

"Andrea is banned from ever stepping foot in this shop again," he snarled.

"What? Why?"

"I can't believe you need me to state the obvious. First,

Andrea messes up her A-levels because of all the hours she spends at this place. Then, thanks to your influence, no doubt, she gets arrested. Arrested."

"Now, it's not like she was charged. They let her go with a caution," Holly said, trying to keep her tone even to avoid escalation, although it was probably already past that. Several customers had poked their heads around the door only to disappear again at the sight of Mr Abbot, hands on hips, staring down a pregnant Holly. Had he been that tall the last time she met him, she wondered? She couldn't remember him being so tall, but then he'd never been shouting directly at her before.

"I found out at the dentist. Did you know that? My dentist. There I was thinking I was going to have a quick clean and check for cavities, and instead, I hear about how my daughter is the talk of the town for getting herself arrested up in London."

"I told Drey she needed to tell you," Holly said, lifting her hands in defence. He couldn't possibly think she was to blame for this, couldn't he? If anything, he should thank her for the fact they picked her up, but this didn't seem the right time to mention that. "She assured me she had told you."

"I've always thought it ridiculous, the amount of pressure you put on her. You and that other woman before you. Relying on her to run your businesses because you're too lazy to do it yourself. No wonder she didn't get the exam results we expected. Well, let's see how you manage without her."

In the split second he turned to move out of the door, something inside Holly snapped. Perhaps it was the fact he had mentioned Maud or that he had accused her of taking advantage of Drey when she had done everything she could not to do that. No, Holly was not taking this. Not today.

"You talk about me putting pressure on her." The words

were out of her mouth before she could stop herself. "What about you? What about the pressure you put on her?"

Mr Abbot turned as if in slow motion. If possible, he was getting even bigger with every second it took to face her.

"What did you say?"

"You heard me," Holly said, straightening her back as much as the baby bump would allow. "You come here to my shop, telling me what to do in my business, thinking you can shout at me like I'm some child. Why didn't she ring you? Did you ask yourself that? Did you ask yourself why, when it was the middle of the night, and she was in trouble, it wasn't her dad she went to for help? *You* put too much pressure on her. You're the one who doesn't even see how amazing she is."

"I know exactly how amazing my daughter is. And how smart. And I see exactly how she wastes all her potential weighing out bags of sweets day in and day out."

"If you know her that well, then why didn't she call you?"

"Because you've brainwashed her in this place. You and that old woman."

"If you even—"

"Holly, please don't." Holly looked past Mr Abbot's bulging eyes and saw the tear-stained face of Drey behind him. Never had Holly seen her in such a manner. Hunched over, hands wringing out in front of her. By the look of things, she had been crying for hours. "There's no point, Holly. Just leave it."

"Drey," Holly took a step forward, but Mr Abbot was already blocking her route.

"I told you to stay in the car," he hissed at Drey. "I warned you. I told you—"

"This isn't Holly's fault, Dad. It's not. I told you it's not. This was me. This was my fault."

"You're only a child."

"No, I'm not, Dad. I'm not only a child."

"You're my child," he said. For the first time in the conversation, he finally quietened his voice by a fraction, and Holly could feel the shift in the air. Drey took a step closer to her father.

"Holly's right. I can't talk to you about things. I wanted to ring you. I did. You were the person I wanted, but then I knew what you'd be like. How you'd start yelling and making me feel worse than I already did, and I didn't need that. I'm sorry. I am sorry, Dad. But please don't make me give up the shop. Whether you like it or not, I am an adult, and where I live and work is my decision. Don't make me choose between the shop and you. You don't want to do that."

"You'd choose this place over your own family?" Mr Abbot snorted in disgust. Even Holly was surprised by what she was hearing, but the look on Drey's face was just as determined as her father's had been when he first came in.

"I would choose being allowed to be me over being controlled. Yes."

Silence engulfed them—a heavy and dense silence. Drey's cheeks were no longer merely tear-streaked. The tears were once again streaming down them. Silently. Demurely. Her eyes locked on her father as she waited for his reply. In the end, though, it wasn't Drey he looked at. It was Holly.

"I suppose you're pleased about this," he said. "I suppose you're pleased she'd choose you over her own family?"

Of course, she wasn't. Holly was as dumbfounded as Mr Abbot that this would be Drey's response, but at the same time, she could see her young employee had been backed into a corner when all this could probably have been resolved with a cup of tea and a proper conversation. And that was what she was going to say. Or at least words to that effect, but she didn't get a chance to. Because when she opened her mouth to speak, the pain struck again. This time, it was so much more than just a kick. It was unlike anything she had ever felt in her life. And rather than saying anything at all, Holly clutched her side and screamed.

CHAPTER FORTY-FOUR

Holly gasped, trying to suck the scream back in, but it wouldn't stay down. Her eyes were watering, streaming, her jaw clenched against the pain.

"Holly?" Drey pushed past her father to get to Holly's side. "You need to sit down. Is it the baby? Of course, it's the baby. Sit down. I'm calling an ambulance."

Holly took a deep breath in through her nose, preparing for the pain to continue, only it didn't. It had subsided altogether as if the moment had never happened.

She reached her hand across to Drey, who had just grabbed her phone out of her pocket.

"It's fine," she said. "Honestly. It's fine. It's passed now." Drey hovered, her phone still in hand, poised and ready to dial.

"How long have you been having pains like that?"

"Honestly, it's not that bad. I've just been on my feet all day. That's all."

For the first time since she had entered the shop, Drey exchanged a look with her father that didn't translate to the pair wanting to rip each other's throats out. Holly knew exactly what they were thinking. And she also knew they were very definitely wrong.

"No," she said before either of them could suggest it. "I know what you're going to say, but it's not. It's a false alarm, that's all. Braxton Hicks, that's what they call them. Everyone in my antenatal class has had them now. I was starting to feel left out if I'm honest."

She attempted a light-hearted chuckle to reinforce the point, but the pain struck again. It wasn't nearly as bad that time, though, possibly because she was sitting down and got through it without so much as a yelp. However, it didn't go unnoticed.

"That was another one, wasn't it?" Mr Abbot spoke this time. His face was just as serious as when he first entered the shop, although he was a fraction less angry.

"It's just cramps, that's all," Holly said, standing up to show she was completely and utterly fine and definitely not—as they were trying to suggest—about to go into labour. "Honestly, there are other signs besides contractions, you know—lots of other signs. I'm completely fine. Anyway, I'm only thirty-seven weeks, and first babies are almost always late."

Once again, the father and daughter exchanged a look.

"I think you should ring, Ben," Drey said eventually. "Even if it is a false alarm, he'd want to know. He'd want to be kept in the loop."

"Trust me, the last thing Ben wants is me dragging him into another scene when there's absolutely nothing wrong," Holly said. "Besides, this will be over in half an hour, and you'll wonder what you were panicking about."

"Okay then, half an hour it is. Andrea, have you got your phone?"

"Already on it, Dad."

Holly frowned. She was trying to figure out what part of the conversation she had missed when the pain struck again. Yes, they were definitely worse when she was standing. When this one stopped, she would move the seat behind the till. It was likely to break a few health and safety rules given the tiny space behind them, but she couldn't go through all this standing up. And maybe a good sit down was all she needed to stop them altogether. Drey, however, obviously had other ideas as she slipped in behind the till pulling her blue and white striped apron out of her bag.

"You'll have to take over, Dad," she said, handing her father the phone. "So if any customers come in, I can serve."

"Will do. You've made a note of that last one, too?"

"Of course I have."

"Sorry?" Holly said, suddenly feeling like a stranger in her own shop. "What is it you're keeping track of?"

"Your contractions, obviously," Drey said casually as she wiped down the scales and straightened out the scoops.

"What? I told you. They're not contractions. They're Braxton Hicks."

"We heard you," Drey said with a shrug.

"The thing is, if they are Braxton Hicks, then they're not going to get any closer together," Drey's father continued. "So, like you said, we'll wait here for half an hour. Then, we'll go if they're still as regular or further apart. If not, we'll be staying to the point that you need driving to the hospital. Assuming you haven't called someone else to take over from us by this point. I must admit, this is not how I imagined spending my Saturday afternoon."

Mr Abbot's words were cut short when a young family with two pushchairs and a baby in a carrier came in.

Not waiting for her to object or refuse, Mr Abbot picked up the stool and ushered Holly up the stairs.

"We should probably move to the stockroom," he said. "If my timings are right, it's less than a minute until the next contraction, and it's probably best for all of us if you don't have to navigate that impossible staircase during them. Perhaps you should brace yourself."

"Really, all of this is utterly unnecessary. If anything, it's just stre—"

Holly didn't get to finish the last word. All the air left her mouth in a long breath as the same squeezing sensation gripped her abdomen. At least she hadn't screamed that time. That was something.

"Bang on time," Mr Abbot said, and Holly could have sworn a satisfied smirk flickered on the corner of his.

Holly gave herself a second to catch her breath before she spoke. "Like you said, they're not getting any closer, meaning it's fine." She gritted as she forced herself to smile. They might not be getting closer, but that was definitely the longest she had experienced so far. Not that she was going to let them know that.

Across the shop floor, Drey was swiftly dealing with the customers. Holly watched as Mr Abbot's eyes momentarily left the stopwatch and lingered on his daughter.

"She really is an amazing people person," Holly said. "And I'm so lucky to have her here. I know that. I really would never take advantage of her."

The softness that had briefly infiltrated Mr Abbot's features was replaced by his previous hardness.

"Forgive me if I want more for my daughter than slinging sweets into a bag for the rest of her life."

"Then why not just be content to trust her to do something she loves doing now? You said it yourself. She's still so young. Did you know what you wanted to do at eighteen? I didn't. And

I'm sure she'll want much more than this in a couple of years, but it could be a great stepping stone, you know, teaching her to run her own business, that type of thing."

While he didn't reply, Mr Abbot's silent glance down at his phone told Holly what to expect. She inhaled through her nose, pulling in a lungful of air, then blowing it out in a long stream just as they had shown her in the ridiculously priced antenatal classes. Though she was surprised to find it helped. A lot.

"I think they're easing off now," she said, raising her voice a little as the customer left so Drey could hear too. "You guys are probably fine leaving. I'm sure I'll be completely fine."

"Still got another twenty minutes to go," Mr Abbot said.

CHAPTER FORTY-FIVE

"That was a long one," Mr Abbot said, raising his eyebrows as Holly exhaled slowly with a long hiss, trying to maintain as relaxed a look as possible.

"No. It was the same as all the others," Holly lied, offering her most nonchalant shrug, wishing there was just a little more air movement in the room. "Possibly even a bit lighter. I think they're passing."

"They're not. I hate to tell you this, but they're getting closer together. I don't want to rush you or anything, but—"

"There's nothing to rush," Holly said. "If they're getting faster, it's just because they're nearing the end. That's all,"

She sounded convincing to herself. And she was close to believing it when the next jab came. This time biting down on her cheeks wasn't enough to stop her from gasping out of pain.

"That's it. We're going to the hospital. This is ridiculous." This time it wasn't Drey's father speaking, it was Drey.

"Just give me a minute. Give me a minute, and it'll pass," Holly said, trying to stop the beads of sweat that had started budding on her forehead.

"We give you any longer, and you're gonna have this baby of yours on the shop floor."

"Stop now. I'll be fine. I just need to sit down for a minute, that's all."

"You're gonna sit down for a minute, in the car, on the way to the hospital." It was a good retort that Holly probably would have chuckled at had she been in a chuckling mood. Unfortunately, Drey still wasn't done. "Look, if you're not going to think of yourself or the baby, then at least think of the shop. I don't know what the rules are, but I'm fairly certain that if someone has a baby on a sweet shop floor, then there will be all these rules about cleaning crews and health inspectors. We'll probably have to be closed for a week to get through all the red tape. Are you willing to take that risk?"

Holly had never actually looked into what would happen if someone had a baby in the shop, but surely the health inspectors couldn't make her close for that, could they? She barely had time to fix the thoughts when Mr Abbot moved to her side, hooking his arm under hers.

"Andrea, you've got keys to this place, haven't you? Time to lock up."

"I'm on it."

"We need to cash up first," Holly said, suddenly worried about the day's takings sitting in the till.

"Don't worry. I can ring Caroline to come in and do that later. I'll lock up here and be in the car in two minutes."

With a face that was scarily reminiscent of when he had first arrived at the shop, Mr Abbot turned to his daughter.

"If you think you're coming to the hospital with us, you've got another think coming," he said. "I've still not forgotten about the reason I'm here in the first place."

"Well, I'm not leaving Holly on her own with you," Drew replied. "What if she can't get hold of Ben? You can't go into the labour suite with her. You fainted at my birth, remember? And as you keep forgetting, I'm an adult. I can make my own decisions."

At this, Mr Abbot sucked in his cheeks and let out a short hiss.

"Fine, but we are not done talking about this situation."

"I agree, but we will talk about it once we know that Holly and the baby are okay."

In the car, Holly stared at her phone. Sitting down was easier, and the surges had died down a bit. Maybe she could close her eyes in the car. She certainly felt like she needed a nap.

"You know you need to ring Ben," Drey said quietly as they drove out of the village. "He deserves to be there. I can ring him if that's easier?"

Anxiety rippled through Holly, and it wasn't the same as the one that had been afflicting her for the last few hours. A different tension had gripped her, and it was equally painful.

"Ben and I are in a bad place," Holly whispered, feeling the tears well in her eyes. She wiped them away before they could fall, but it didn't stop the next stream from coming. Drey reached out and placed a hand on her shoulders.

"So? Bad times come and go. And so do good times. But this…" She nodded to Holly's bump. "Having this baby, it's only going to happen once, and whatever state yours and Ben's relationship is in, you're going to regret it if you don't allow him to be there. You know that."

Holly sniffed, though it did little to stem the tears now rolling down her cheeks.

She picked up her phone to dial, and a loud sniff from the

front of the car attracted her attention. In the mirror, she exchanged a glance with Mr Abbot, who was also wiping a stray tear from his eye.

"I raised a good one," he said with a glance at his daughter.

CHAPTER FORTY-SIX

"Have you tried him again? You need to keep trying. You need to get hold of him!"

"It's just going straight to voicemail," Drey said.

"Then message him. Email him. You need to get him here!"

Holly Berry was in labour.

The head nurse on duty had confirmed it. Although for a fair amount of time, Holly had refused to believe her.

"How about you do your job, and I do mine," the head nurse replied when Holly asked her to check again. "Unless you want to stick around to clean the room up here after you're done, too?" At this comment, the nurse offered Holly a look that would have made Drey's father cower, and Holly clamped her mouth shut.

"Why would he not be answering his phone?" Holly said, exasperated, as she took the phone away from Drey and looked at the screen. Not that she needed to check anything. Was it really that much of a surprise that Ben wasn't replying? After all, he hadn't even told her he was going up to London. And with three weeks to go, why would he think she was in labour when she had refused to believe it herself? "What about Caroline? And Jamie? Have you got hold of them?"

"Caroline's on her way here. And she's sent Michael to sort the shop before you ask," Drey said. "And she's going to pick up Jamie on the way. They won't be long now. Oh, and they're going to get your mum, too. I didn't know if that was the right thing to do, but the nurses wouldn't let me come in and out on the phone, so I just guessed."

Holly nodded. Jamie and Caroline. And her mum. All were racing to her side in her hour of need. But not Ben. No husband or boyfriend. It wasn't how she imagined having her first baby, but it was a bit too late to think about that now.

"Drey—"

She was about to ask Drey if she could fetch her a cup of water as her tongue felt like a dry flannel had replaced it, but Drey was speaking over her before she could start the sentence properly.

"I'm really sorry about not telling my dad straight away. I know it was stupid. I know I shouldn't have lied. I just knew how he was going to blow up about things. And I'm so sorry you got dragged into it. He didn't mean all those things he said to you. I promise."

Had things been different, Holly could have been furious about how Drey handled the situation. But this wasn't the right time for any anger. Besides, it was clear she had already gone through enough. With a warmth inside her, that was almost distracting her from everything else going on, she reached out and took Drey's hand.

"It's all right. And I'm grateful you felt you could call me."

Drey nodded, watery eyed.

"You don't know it, but you coming to Bourton, running the shop, you changed my life. It's hard to explain, but you did. I would be a complete wreck if you hadn't come along. This baby is very lucky to have you as its mum."

Holly was about to reply how sweet and probably untrue it was for her to say that when pain shot right the way down her spine.

"Christ!" Every muscle in her body clenched tight, from her jaw to her toes. "I don't think my body is ready to do this," she said, grabbing Drey's hand.

"You're fine. It's going to be fine," Drey replied.

"How?" Holly was panting as she spoke. "I don't know what I'm doing. I can't even keep a relationship going. What type of life will this baby have with me as its mother? It's going to hate me."

"You're getting yourself stressed," Drey said, prising her hand out of Holly's grip.

"Of course, I'm stressed. I'm about to have a baby."

"You need to breathe. You need to focus on your breathing. Breathe."

"I am breathing. I wouldn't be able to shout if I wasn't brea—" But Holly couldn't finish her sentence for two reasons. The first reason was that she was hit with another sudden contraction. There was no denying it now. They were contractions, and this baby was definitely going to make an appearance into the world soon. But also, at that exact moment, the door swung open.

"The cavalry's here!" Bounding through the double doors were Caroline, Jamie, and her mother.

At the sight of all the women, Holly's eyes filled with tears that weren't from emotional or physical pain for the first time in days.

"I brought the snacks," Caroline said, holding a tote back

bulging at the seams with crisps and chocolate. "Labour makes you bloody ravenous. Or at least it did with me."

"And I brought something to wet the baby's head," Jamie said, holding up a bottle of bubbly.

"And I just brought a hand to hold," Wendy said, locking her eyes on her daughter and causing Holly's chest to squeeze so tightly her breath stuttered.

"What the hell is all this?" The surly head nurse who had suggested Holly would like to clean up the mess was back in the room, looking even more impatient than she had before. "This is a hospital ward. There are patients here."

"We're family," Jamie piped up. "We want to be here for the birth,"

The woman tightened her lips, which twisted and corkscrewed.

"All family?"

"Well, I'm her mother," Wendy piped up indignantly. "I'm not going anywhere."

"And I'm her sister," Caroline responded without missing a beat. "We're all her sisters."

"All family," Jamie added.

The nurse cast her scathing eye around them all. There wasn't a similarity between the four of them, from eye colour, hair colour, or skin tone. Holly watched the muscles on the nurse's jaw twitch and knew that any second now, she would kick some of them out at least, but the door opened for the third time.

"Holly?"

Despite the fact that Holly had only ever seen the woman once before, she recognised her instantly. Possibly due to the midwife's uniform. Possibly because of how much she had heard about her in the last few months.

"Faye?"

Giles' younger sister stared back at Holly as the rest of the room watched on in confusion.

"Do you know the patient?" the strict nurse said to Faye, momentarily directing her anger away from Holly and her friends.

"Vaguely. She's a friend of my brother."

"Well, she insists that all these women are family and should stay here at the birth."

Holly had zero idea how much Giles had told Faye about her if he had said anything at all, but she struggled to believe anyone could think this rag-tag group was related.

"Yes, absolutely," Faye said with certainty, making even Holly believe her. "Can't you see the similarities? Yes, all family."

"See?" Jamie sighed with accentuated exasperation.

Unimpressed with this response, the nurse offered yet another scowl.

"Fine, but only one of you can stay when the doctor gets here and I will be kicking you all out if there's any noise."

"Noise?" Jamie piped up again. "You realise she's having a baby?"

With a huff that reminded Holly more of a headteacher than a nurse, the woman turned on her heel and left.

"Thank you," Holly mouthed to Faye.

"No problem," she replied with a grin. "Now, let's have a look at where we are at."

Breathing a momentary sigh of relief, Holly shifted slightly in her bed.

As Faye examined her, four women were looking at her. Four amazing women, almost all were wearing the same expression of delighted disbelief. Even with the throbbing spasms that were shooting through her belly and the waves of anxiety gripping her, she thought about the future. Holly couldn't help but take a moment to smile. Jamie was right. They were more than friends; they were family. And if they hadn't been before this, they certainly would be now.

Faye popped her head back up.

"Well, I think we should probably get the doctor and get on with it," she said with a big grin.

CHAPTER FORTY-SEVEN

Holly Berry had a baby.

She had trouble getting the words to sink in, but it was true. Holly Berry had a baby. An amazing, beautiful baby, all pink and crinkled, with a scrunched-up face and a smell so sweet and intense she wondered how she had survived without it before. The moment the child was placed upon Holly's chest, it had been love at first sight. Not that soppy rom-com, *he's the one*, type of love at first sight. No, this was something different. Something instinctive.

The birth hadn't been fun, but she'd had her mum by her side while her friends waited outside and it was over now. Perhaps it was a good thing that she'd not managed to get through to Ben, she thought, as she rocked the wrinkled newborn in her arms, because there wasn't a thing she'd change about what had happened. Holly had been surrounded by people she loved, and Holly was in love, totally and utterly. While some might look at her life and consider it a train wreck, she couldn't be happier.

"Have you picked a name yet?" Caroline asked, staring at

the baby. It was strange to have so many people staring at her, not talking, just watching a little bundle in her arms, but Holly didn't care in the slightest. Why should she? She was staring too.

"I think so, but I should probably check with Ben," Holly said, not wanting him to miss out on that too.

"Pfft, let him choose the middle name," Jamie said. "You're the one who did all the hard work."

Hard work? Holly thought as she stared at her daughter. Yes, it had been, yet somehow it felt exactly like it was meant to have done.

She lifted her gaze away from the baby to look at her mother, whose eyes had been glistening with tears almost permanently from the moment she arrived at the hospital.

"Oh my goodness, I need to ring your father. He'll want to be here."

Wiping the tears from her cheeks, Wendy kissed the baby on the forehead and followed it up with a quick kiss for Holly before she scuttled off out the door, already dialling Arthur.

"Talking about fathers, I think it's probably time I faced mine." Drey was still standing in the corner of the room, having been there the entire time. "Congratulations. She is perfect."

Caroline slipped her arm inside Jamie's. "If it's okay with you, we should probably head off too," she said. "I'm sure you need some time to get to know your little girl, but if you want one of us to stay…" Holly was only half listening to them. How was it possible that something so tiny could command so much attention? It wasn't like she was even doing anything. They were just together.

"Holly?" Caroline and Jamie were looking at her expectedly. "Do you want us to stay?"

It didn't take much consideration for Holly to answer.

"No, it's fine, you go. We'll be completely fine, won't we,

little girl?" She leaned forward ever so slightly to kiss her friends on the cheeks before turning her attention back to the baby.

"And remember to give us a call when you need a lift home," Jamie said. "Fin is desperate to meet her, and he's already set up the car seat in your car, so you don't have to worry about that."

In truth, Holly hadn't worried about anything outside of this room at all since she first set eyes on her daughter. It all seemed so far away and distant. She knew it soon wouldn't, though. Car seats, nappies, milk reflux, and sleepless nights were probably just hours away. She wasn't under any illusion that this was going to be easy. There was still the whole mess with Ben to sort out, not to mention her feelings for Giles. But for now, even that couldn't affect her. She was going to make the most of every precious second before real life intruded.

Tiredness hit quite suddenly, and with it, the knowledge that Holly had no idea what the time was. It was dark outside, but that was all she knew. Still, it didn't matter. A wide yawn caused tears to prick her eyes, and she was busy debating whether it was better to put the baby in the crib so she could get a little rest or just keep holding her when a male figure slipped into the room.

"I am so sorry. I am so sorry. Oh my God, did I really miss it?"

Holly blinked.

"Ben?"

"First, I lost my phone, and I just had a feeling that I should get back, then the traffic—"

"Ben, stop! It doesn't matter," Holly said. "Just come and meet your daughter."

"We have a daughter? I have a daughter?" Ben's face flushed with love as he swept up against the bed. "Is everything all right? Is she healthy? She looks healthy. Does she look healthy?"

"She's perfectly healthy," Holly replied, finding it strange to be the calm one, given the normal nature of their relationship.

"Can I hold her?"

It was a question no one, not even Wendy had asked. And Holly wanted to say no. If she'd had her way, she would've stayed like that, with the baby curled up on her chest, just the two of them for at least the next three months. But Ben was her father, and she wanted to respect that.

"This is your daddy," Holly said, holding the baby out for Ben to take. "Daddy, this is Hope."

Ben's jaw was still hanging open, so much so that it took him a second to realise what Holly had said.

"Hope?"

"If you're okay with it?"

Ben didn't respond as he cradled the baby back and forth in his arms. Was that what she looked like? Holly wanted to know. Absorbed by such complete and utter adoration. Probably.

"Hope," Ben said again. "I like it. I really like it. Hope Thornbury."

"That hasn't been decided yet," Holly said with a little force.

"Okay," Ben grinned. "We can work on that, but I like Hope. It is perfect."

That was it. The first hurdle was overcome. It wasn't just a name. Holly felt in the pit of her gut. It was her and Ben acting together as parents. It was a name they both agreed on, but it signified so much more than that. It signified that they could do this. They were going to be okay.

"We are going to need to talk about living arrangements and things," Ben said, his practical nature seeping into the moment.

"I know we do, but not now. Not now."

The truth was that Holly already knew what she would say, and she didn't want to ruin the moment. Not for Ben. Not for her. They would talk when they got home. And she would stay at Ben's tonight if that was what he wanted. After all, she wasn't going to be parted from Hope. It was only fair he was offered the same opportunity. For a minute, they stayed there in silence, which only broke when Hope emitted a low grizzling.

"I think she wants her mama back," Ben said, leaning over and placing Hope back into Holly's arms. "Do you need anything? Food? Drink?"

Holly cast a slight smile up to Ben. "Some water would be great," she gestured to the empty jug on the bedside table, at which point Ben promptly picked it up.

"More water coming up."

With a last beaming smile at Hope, he moved to the door, only for it to swing open in front of him. Rather than shifting to the side to let whoever it was into the room, Ben turned rigid on the spot. His fist balled at his side and shook with a tremble so violently that Holly could see it from her bed.

"Ben, is everything all right?" Holly said, the serenity of only moments before shifting slightly.

But Ben didn't turn and face her. "What the hell are you doing here?" he spat at the doorway. "Get out. Get out now."

And Holly knew exactly who he was talking to.

CHAPTER FORTY-EIGHT

"How the hell did you get in here?" Ben snarled as he blocked the doorway, not letting him enter the room. For a split second, Holly feared they would end up fighting. It wouldn't have been the first time that had happened over her. Yet Giles shifted to the side ever so slightly, just so that he came into Holly's line of sight. Unlike Ben, Holly didn't need to ask how Giles had been allowed onto the ward. Faye was probably also the reason he knew she was there in the first place.

"She's perfect. You look perfect," Giles said, gazing at Holly, who, for the first time since Hope had arrived, considered what she must actually look like. Dressed in her hospital gown, dishevelled hair plastered to her head by sweat. Perfect didn't seem quite right. Although the way Giles was looking at her, he could have been staring at the Mona Lisa.

"Are you okay?" he said, still not moving past the boundary Ben was holding fast. "Was everything okay?"

"I'm fine," Holly replied. "Tired, but fine."

Giles nodded. "Okay, I should leave you to get some rest. I just wanted to say. Well, you know…" Holly was fairly sure she knew. She knew exactly what he was saying, and a deep pulse squeezed her heart.

At that moment, she wanted nothing more than to leave it there. To ignore everything and deal only with Hope, but she knew that sooner or later, she had to face reality. Maybe Ben turning up late at the same time as Giles was fate telling her she should deal with it now. That way, she would leave the hospital, and all these worries about what she should do would be past her. It would be her and Hope and a future of her choosing.

"I think you should both come in. And take a seat," she said, looking back at Ben as she spoke. He didn't move, but she nodded softly, and she knew there was no way he would put up a fight in front of Hope even if she didn't understand a word they were both saying.

The problem with asking them to take a seat was that there was only one, and so while Giles dropped into the tub chair next to her, Ben perched himself on the end of the bed. Holly placed Hope in the crib next to her as much as she didn't want to. She was fast asleep, but Holly still felt a longing to keep her close.

"We need to address this," she said. "And I need you both to be here, to listen to what I'm saying. To hear what I'm saying." She drew a deep breath in. She thought labour was tough, but this would be much harder. And the outcome? Well, there was no way she could make everyone happy, but the truth was, they weren't all equal in this. There was one person whose happiness she had to put first. Herself.

"Ben." She looked at the man whose baby she had just brought into the world, who she had near enough lived with for the last six months. Who had tried marriage counselling in the earliest stages of their relationship to try to make it work. But that was the crux of it. Should they really have had to work so hard to make it work that early on?

"Ben, I love you so much. I do, but I don't think we bring out the best in each other, and if we're honest, if Hope hadn't arrived on the scene, then you and I would have been over long ago."

"I don't believe that," Ben said, in what was probably his most managerial voice possible.

"Yes, you do. You might not want to, but we wouldn't have lasted. We were both in a place where we wanted the happy ever after, and on paper, we were perfect. But paper isn't good enough for us." He opened his mouth to object, but Holly wasn't done yet, and she wasn't going to stop until she had said everything she needed to. "We could force ourselves to be together. We could do that for the sake of our friends and our friendship because when it comes down to it, that's what you are. You are one of my best friends. You make me feel safe. You make me feel supported. You have done everything for this baby and me. And maybe that's enough for some people. Maybe it should be enough for me… I know it should be…" She didn't want to say the rest, but she didn't need to. Ben was already there with it.

"But it's not enough for you," he said.

"I wish it was," Holly said, feeling the heat behind her eyes. "I really wish it was enough. And nobody can't say we didn't try. We did. And I am so thankful that I get to keep you in my life as Hope's father and, hopefully, in time, as my friend. My best friend again."

Ben sniffed and looked down at the ground. His jaw was locked, but his chin nodded ever so slightly. He understood, just like she had known, or rather hoped he would. And so that left Giles.

As she looked at him, he offered her a grin. A tiny flicker of a smile, although she could see the fear twinkling in his eyes.

Still, that didn't stop her from reciprocating his smile as if it were a reflex action that she couldn't control.

"You," she said, unable to even say his name. "I don't think I will ever understand you—bad boy image, good boy image. But, these past few months, you have been there for me in ways I would never have expected. And I know that if we were together, every day spent with you would be an adventure."

His smile softened, but the light in his eyes grew a fraction brighter.

"I would make sure it was."

"I know. But I have a big enough adventure waiting for me," Holly said, nodding toward Hope. "And not understanding you might be fun for a while, but I can't put that ahead of what's best for my daughter, which is stability." Giles' smile dropped, and his forehead creased as if he didn't know what she was saying. That was it. She had said everything she needed to.

"Just to get this right, you're not choosing either of us?" Giles said.

"I'm choosing you *both*, as friends," Holly said.

"So you want him in your life, too?" Ben said.

"If that's possible. If that's not, then I understand and accept that."

Given how calm Ben had been through her previous speech, she was surprised by the confusion he now displayed.

"Why would you do that?" he asked, the volume of his voice notably louder than before. "I could understand if you chose him over me, but to choose to be on your own… it doesn't make sense."

She could see the wounded sheen in his eyes, and she wished more than anything she could fix that, but Holly knew she couldn't.

"She's doing it because it's what's right for her," Giles said.

"I get it. She's looking after number one." He snorted, an attempt at anger, but Holly could see the pain he was trying to cover. "Looking after number one. Funny, this is the first time I haven't done that, and what do you know? I've ended up on the losing side."

Holly wanted to tell him that he wasn't on the losing side. That maybe they could all come out as friends, but she knew she couldn't.

"I'm sorry," she said. "I'm sorry to do this to you both. I really am. But this is the only way that's fair. I'm choosing me. And I'm choosing Hope."

As if she already knew her name, Hope shifted in the crib, her mouth moving in a manner that already had Holly hopelessly in love. Holly Berry didn't look at the men again. Instead, she picked up her daughter from the crib and let the rest of the world slip away. Whatever happened, Holly and Hope would have a future full of love and adventure. So much of both. And she couldn't wait for that future to start.

The End

NEXT IN THIS SERIES

First off, book 5 ***is*** coming. However, due to your amazing support for this series it has been picked up by Boldwood Books who are going to takeover the publishing.

I love being an indie self-publisher, it affords me better creative control and flexibility. Unfortunately it does mean there are audiences that are closed to me, particularly those that like to purchase from good old bricks and mortar bookshops. Boldwood Books aims to fix this. That's right, you will soon be able to pick up my books in stores (probably with snazzy new covers).

So why the delay? Well Boldwood need to re-release books 1 to 4 before they go straight in and launch book 5. So while it is exciting, it sadly means you will have to wait til October 2023 to find out how Holly and Hope are getting along.

Never fear though, make sure you are signed to my newsletter or to my Facebook page and you will get a few sneaky snippets along the way, plus details the moment the book is available.

Now if the wait is too distressing for you I do have another series that I think you will love releasing sooner.

IT'S NEVER TO LATE

A *Lonely Hearts Bookclub* Novel

She thinks he is uptight and controlling.

He thinks she is frivolous and irresponsible.

The perfect ingredients for a heart-warming romantic comedy.

Fleur Fisher is a hopeless romantic and has had her heart broken more times than she can count. Having come to the conclusion that Mr. Right isn't out there after all, it seems somewhat fated that she should stumble upon the ***Lonely Hearts Book Club***.

Cynical divorce lawyer **Henry Gibson** believes all relationships are doomed to fail, but while he may be content to let love pass him by his grandmother, Edith, most certainly isn't and she is constantly on the lookout for potential granddaughters-in-law.

Busy navigating a new town, new friendships and unexpected visits from her sisters, Fleur is not interested in finding love again, and even if she were she is certain her fellow book clubber's pompous and arrogant grandson is not who she is looking for, even if he is devilishly handsome.

As Fleur and Henry continue to cross paths with increasing frequency will they be able to see past their differences or will realisation come too late for this mismatched pair.

Perfect for fans of Jill Mansell, Milly Johnson and Heidi Swain, this delightful *enemies to lovers* romance is guaranteed to restore your faith in true love and leave you feeling warm and fuzzy.

ACKNOWLEDGMENTS

To Cherie, whose beautiful covers really help this series standout, thank you as always.

Thank you to Victoria for her diligent editing.

Huge thanks to the amazing team of proofreaders, especially Kath, Ana, Yolanda and John who have done their utmost to track down those persistent typos that are hell-bent on ruining your reading pleasure.

Lastly, thank you to all you readers who have taken Holly into your heart. I hope very much that her antics continue to bring you joy.

ABOUT THE AUTHOR

Hannah Lynn is an award-winning novelist. Publishing her first book, *Amendments* – a dark, dystopian speculative fiction novel, in 2015, she has since gone on to write *The Afterlife of Walter Augustus* – a contemporary fiction novel with a supernatural twist – which won the 2018 Kindle Storyteller Award and Gold Medal for Best Adult Fiction Ebook at the IPPY Awards, as well as the delightfully funny and poignant *Peas and Carrots series.*

Her latest works include retellings of classic Greek myths and saw her win her second IPPY Gold Medal for the first book in her *Grecian Women Series*, the heart-wrenching *Athena's Child.*

Born in 1984, Hannah grew up in the Cotswolds, UK. After graduating from university, she spent ten years as a teacher of physics, first in the UK, then in Thailand, Malaysia, Austria and Jordan. It was during this time, inspired by the imaginations of the young people she taught, she began writing short stories for children, before moving on to adult fiction.

Nowadays you will most likely find her busy writing at home with her husband and daughter, surrounded by a clowder of cats.

STAY IN TOUCH

To keep up-to-date with new publications, tours and promotions, or if you are interested in being a beta reader for future novels, or having the opportunity to enjoy pre-release copies please follow me:

Website: hannahlynnauthor.com

Alternatively sign up to my newsletter and receive a free book.

Sign-up to Newsletter

REVIEW

As an independent author, I do not have the mega resources of a big publishing house, but what I do have is something even more powerful – all of you readers. Your ability to offer social proof to my books through your reviews is invaluable to me and helps me to continue writing.

So if you enjoyed reading ***High Hopes at the Sweet Shop of Second Chances***, please take a few moments to leave a review or rating on Amazon, Bookbub or Goodreads. It need only be a sentence or two, but it means so much to me.

Thank you.

Printed in Great Britain
by Amazon

17747209R00154